心笛
王潤華
瘂弦
黎漢傑　編

風
媒

集

周策縱

翻譯詩集

周策縱攝於陌地生棄園門前。

前言

心笛（浦麗琳）

　　這書冊中的英詩中譯，是照周策縱教授身後遺留下來早年譯詩的影印手寫原稿，不加修飾，以原貌打字編排出版。

　　二〇〇九年，周教授長女周聆蘭由北加州回到「陌地生」城，「民遁」路的「棄園」清理她父母故居留剩下的雜物，將一些多餘的周公舊作和紙張信封寄來給我。其中有一堆四寸厚的、早年周公英詩中譯零亂的稿件影印本，和周公在二〇〇四年寫給名詩人瘂弦信的影印。信中示出周公將自己的譯詩稿已寄給瘂弦，托瘂弦在臺灣代找出版社出版譯詩集。我即向名編輯瘂弦探聽，知悉當年他沒能找到合適的出版社為老師的譯詩集成功出版。

　　譯詩稿，是周教授早年滴滴心血和生命的結晶，不能出版，太可惜了。詩緣書緣，我決定要想辦法推動出版這位昔日白馬社周公的譯詩集。

　　瘂弦電話裡曾說，他退休後更無能找到出版社相助出版。誰能呢？腦海中立刻浮起最能幫助周教授出書的人，周教授生前得意門生詩人王潤華教授。潤華曾在周老師體弱病中，特為老師的新詩集《胡說草》出版成書。後來他又熱心地自我手中接棒，將周教授幾十年前就想出版的《海外新詩鈔》，於二〇一〇年，在臺灣精美地出版成功。他對周老師的敬愛，一直讓我敬佩感動。

　　我於是和聆蘭通電話，告訴她寄來的盒中有她父親早年沒能出

版的譯詩舊稿，及我與瘂弦通電話後的想法，說我想找潤華教授幫忙出版。得到聆蘭同意，我寫信並打越洋電話給那時在臺灣元智大學任院長的王潤華教授，請他幫忙出版譯詩事宜。潤華教授一口答應。我便將手中的譯稿對查整理影印妥，航寄臺灣。並囑潤華教授直接向瘂弦教授索取當年周教授寄給瘂弦的那份詩稿。

潤華不久後被馬來西亞的南方大學學院請去當副校長，工作更是萬分繁忙。出版譯詩集的事只好暫擱。但每年過年節時我們都會通電郵，主題是出版周教授譯詩的事。終於，潤華校長發給我好消息，說他請到香港的一位弟子協助，設法先把詩稿請人打字。我們幸有香港的黎漢傑君大力幫忙，他前前後後，辛勞地探聽出版社及試著申請獎助金，並將譯詩稿件用不同的次序和方法重新編排，還代表我們出面接洽秀威出版社、商討一切繁瑣的大小事宜，辛勞萬分。

周策縱教授自一九三七年起開始英詩中譯，幾十年來陸續零星地將英詩譯成中文詩，在那還沒有網路的時代，他所付出的心血可想而知。如今這些譯詩終能結集出版，為周策縱教授完成他早年的一個心願，是值得慶幸的。在此，我要深深感謝潤華和漢傑的功勞。也感謝對這集子的出版有貢獻的每一位。

心笛二〇一六年十月於南加州

風媒集自序

從小孩子的時候起，我也曾有過多少壯志和願心，無論是實際的或是空想的，平凡的或是光怪陸離的，哪一樣沒有？只是從來不曾想到要翻譯什麼新詩。

我還不認識字的時候，姐姐就教會我背熟了《對子書》、《唐詩三百首》、和《千字詩》裡面的句子。後來發覺，爸爸要老師首先教我的是《聖經》，以後唸「人，口，耳，刀，弓，牛，羊……」我十二三歲時最初在報紙上和雜誌上發表的作品也是詩。這樣看來，我和詩從小就有了密切的關係了。可是也就從那時候起，我就有了一種動機，總想把詩戒掉，像一個在道德上和衛生上有了深痛的覺悟的人立志要戒掉鴉片煙一般。我寧願談戰略，搞政治，評論政策和國事，鼓吹時代思潮，或者研究自然科學，寫小說或劇本，什麼都高興，只是絕對不想做詩，更不想譯詩。龔定庵（自珍）那許多「戒詩」的詩曾經給過我深刻的印象。

但是這是真的我？興趣卻有點兒矛盾。我雖然每次寫過一些詩後就反悔，卻從來不討厭「看」詩，而是喜歡「聽」我爸爸讀詩或談詩。一個不願吃鴉片煙的人卻喜歡躺在坑上聞聞香氣，這當然是夠危險的了。我中學時代寫了一千多首詩，正式從這種矛盾的心情裡擠出來的。我終究沒法兒「解除這蠱惑了我許久的符咒」。

後來我又讀了好些西洋的詩，我發現這個世界上的詩的花園多

的很，每個詩園裡都有許多美麗的花朵。我雖然自己不想去做一個園丁，可是往往信步走過那些花園時，有時也不免偷偷的摘下一些零花剩草，或者在地上拾起些沒人注意的落了的花瓣，藏在衣襟裡，想拿回去向朋友們誇耀。——這就是我譯的這些小詩。他們不只來自一個花園，他們原來生長在各種不同的土壤裡，開放在各種不同的角落裡。他們不一定都是頂偉大的或頂好的；只是因為當我走過他們身旁時，投合過我當時的偏好，曾經引起過我注目，曾經感動過我一次或多次，我就顧不了別的，居然把他們譯出來了，把他們採摘回來了。我明明知道：花朵是不可摘的，詩是不能譯的。我「採摘了他底花瓣，卻並沒有時得他底義」。我恐怕這帶回來的花瓣早已失去了那原有的顏色和香氣。但是讀者啊，我已經盡了我底心了，除了這，我還能做什麼呢？

東風吹來了，滿園丁裡的花給吹散了，不同園裡的花朵無計畫的，無目的的給吹在一起了。路旁人咒罵這無情的風，這沒有天才的風，摧殘了那嬌嫩可愛的花容。然而這不討你的風卻盡了個媒婆的職務。從前創造社的人，為了譏諷文學研究會，就說：翻譯只是個媒婆，創作才是處女。但媒婆底職務又有什麼可懺惶的呢？風沒帶來美，它卻希望在詩底紅繩下傳播些種子，讓我們詩園裡將來能開出我的花朵，結出我的果實。這開花結果原是讀者自己底事。「一個孩子底自願就是風底自願。」譯者底志願也只是一個「風底志願」罷了。

真的，我在園裡拾起了一些花瓣，就問她們做我底人。但是她們漲紅了臉不答我，我卻不能忍心把她們放下，我是要「尋遍花蕊，想找到可能長著一顆心的幽境。」

一九五七於安娜堡

編輯凡例

　　周策縱先生為著名漢學家，兼擅古典與現代詩詞，是現代難得
的通儒。周公生前偶有翻譯外國詩人作品，部分譯作亦曾公開發
表。本書按照周公遺稿，稍加整理，其餘或已散佚，或尚待追尋。
書稿現存翻譯詩作數量約一百二十餘首，長篇短調皆有；所涉獵的
詩人，旁及歐美各國，更有部分乃當時新進冒起作家，可證周公慧
眼識見。

　　本書體例略作說明如下：

一、本書盡可能保持原貌，文字上除錯別字必須修定外，不作修改。
二、本書以書稿所譯詩人為單位，同一詩人之作品，按題目筆畫順
　　序放置於同一章節。
三、本書次第以詩人中文譯名排列，先以英文字母，繼以中文筆畫
　　順序。無名氏之詩作，則放置最後。
四、本書原有注釋、附錄一概保留，編者則按具體情況斟酌補上缺
　　文或說明，並以【編者按】標示以便識別。
五、書稿簡體字統一用繁體字，日期統一用中國數字。
六、本書闕舛之處在所難免，還望方家不吝指正。

目次

A・E・休士曼（A. E. Housman）

山花

我辛苦種了些山花，
便把牠們帶到了市場；
又不情願地給帶回家；
牠顏色卻還沒受傷。

於是我到處播種牠，
讓同樣的人去尋求，
那時我已長眠在花下
已是具無名的屍首。
有的種子會餵了野鳥，
有的會給風霜凋零，
但總有幾顆很碰巧
會開出那孤另的星星。

年年野外總有花開，
到綠葉扶疏的船春天，

不幸的人也有花戴，
雖然我永別了人間。

一九五五年四月十一日夜，參照聞一多譯文。

I Hoed and Trenched and Weeded

I hoed and trenched and weeded,
And took the flowers to fair:
I brought them home unheeded;
The hue was not the wear.

So up and down I sow them
For lads like me to find,
When I shall lie below them,
A dead man out of mind.

Some seed the birds devour,
And some the season mars,
But here and there will flower,
The solitary stars,

And fields will yearly bear them
As light-leaved spring comes on,
And luckless lads will wear them
When I am dead and gone.

他們說我底詩悲哀

他們說我底詩悲哀：
這一點也不奇怪；
它短促的節律概括了憂愁和永恆之淚，
他們不屬於我而是屬於人類。

這是為了一切當未出生的
受苦難的人們而作的
讓他們困苦時去吟賞，
我自己卻沒有悲傷。

一九五三年七月二十六日夜

　　按休士曼自己認為受莎士比亞、海涅及英格蘭與蘇格蘭民歌影
響很深。而他取法於拉丁抒情詩的地方，則表現於他底簡練和緊
湊。他底詩常常於省略不說的場合說出了更多的意境，充滿了「雄

辯滔滔的沉默」（eloquent silence），和一種不信宗教的憂鬱感，但他自己卻否認這種深刻的憂鬱感是起源於悲觀主義，他認為他這種情緒，像華滋華斯底一般，是由於聽到了「人性底沉鬱的音樂」（the still, sad music of humanity）所致，他大部分的詩都反映像莎士比亞對人生悲悼的態度：

> 一場黃金般少年男女都要像掃煙囪的人，同歸於灰燼。
> Golden lads and girl all must, as chimney- sweepers, come to dust

他底詩也和莎翁底十四行的一樣，時常把那轉瞬而逝的可怕的「時間」（Time）做主題。Mark Van Doren論莎翁十四行詩的一段話似乎也可用到休斯曼底詩上去。愛德納‧米勒（Edna St‧Vincent Millay）在一九二二年講到休士曼時說：「人們都說，從來沒人見到過他，說他活著像一個影子，還沒有被發現就消失了。」（They say nobody ever sees him, that he goes along like a shadow and in lost before he' found）

They Say My Verse Is Sad

They say my verse is sad: no wonder;
Its narrow measure spans
Tears of eternity, and sorrow,
Not mine, but man's.

This is for all ill-treated fellows
Unborn and unbegot,
For them to read when they're in trouble
And I am not.

西方

在那荒原和山峰底遠方
——同志啊，你莫向西方眺望——
落日已蒸釀天地的美酒
匆匆飲乾了殘餘的白晝。

只有長雲和孤松在留戀
守望著快沉默的地平線，
遠遠地，暮色蒼茫又明顯
直達到黃昏無底的深淵。
於今啊全國人民底兒女
都橫眉向西方驀然回首，
當他遙望到海天底邊際，
便有永恆沉思和歎息。

宇宙多大啊，可安息，流浪，
有故家的歡愉，海外無常，
有戰鬥和歸田，也有清談，
有大塊吃肉，縱酒的伙伴。
但如我面對黃昏的天空
就不禁靜望西方面容，
而我底同志卻踱去踱來，
沉默地在我底身邊徘徊。

同志啊，你別眺望著西方：
它將使你底心跳出胸膛！
把你思緒引得墮落沉埋
墮落到落日底界線以外。

青年啊，那兒怕是那大海，
從那裡，你我曾給救出來，
但是我們雖已給撈起來
怕終究要在那海裡淹死。
不要早把你底心靈送別
那迷人的海岸邊往下跳，
也別讓那游泳者把衣裳
遺留在這黃昏的沙灘上。

你我行色太匆匆，走不到
那荒廢了的海濱和波濤；

別人所見到的暮色蒼茫，
我們不能使牠再放光芒。

宇宙到處有安息或流浪
還早呢，如果要回到家鄉；
在地球上站牢你底腳跟，
讓我們勉強把故鄉忘情。

自從你我給灑布在空中
我們將長久陌生不相逢；
但骨肉的友情至美優良，
同志啊，你不要望著西方。

一九五五年四月

The West

Beyond the moor and the mountain crest
—Comrade, look not on the west—
The sun is down and drinks away
From air and land the lees of day.
The long cloud and the single pine

Sentinel the ending line,

And out beyond it, clear and wan,

Reach the gulfs of evening on.

The son of woman turns his brow

West from forty countries now,

And, as the edge of heaven he eyes,

Thinks eternal thoughts, and sighs.

Oh wide's the world, to rest or roam,

With change abroad and cheer at home,

Fights and furloughs, talk and tale,

Company and beef and ale.

But if I front the evening sky

Silent on the west look I,

And my comrade, stride for stride,

Paces silent at my side,

Comrade, look not on the west:

'Twill have the heart out of your breast;

'Twill take your thoughts and sink them far,

Leagues beyond the sunset bar.

Oh lad, I fear that yon's the sea

Where they fished for you and me,

And there, from whence we both were ta'en,

You and I shall drown again.

Send not on your soul before

To dive from that beguiling shore,

And let not yet the swimmer leave

His clothes upon the sands of eve.

Too fast to yonder strand forlorn

We journey, to the sunken bourn,

To flush the fading tinges eyed

By other lads at eventide.

Wide is the world, to rest or roam,

And early 'tis for turning home:

Plant your heel on earth and stand,

And let's forget our native land.

When you and I are split on air

Long we shall be strangers there;

Friends of flesh and bone are best;

Comrade, look not on the west.

我二十一歲的時候

我二十一歲的時候

聽到一個聰明人說：

「你可獻出金錢，

可不要獻出你底心；

你可給別人珍珠和紅玉，

卻要保持你底幻想自由。」
可是我那時還只有二十一歲，
這對我都白說了。

我二十一歲的時候
又聽到他說：
「你真誠的深心
終不會白白地獻了，
它會得到許多的歡息的報酬，
也會換來無窮的悔恨。」
現在我是二十二歲了，
我發覺這是真的啊，真的啊。

一九五三年五月二十七日

When I Was One-and-Twenty

When I was one-and-twenty
I heard a wise man say,
"Give crowns and pounds and guineas
But not your heart away;
Give pearls away and rubies

But keep your fancy free."
But I was one-and-twenty,
No use to talk to me.
When I was one-and-twenty
I heard him say again,
"The heart out of the bosom
Was never given in vain;
'Tis paid with sighs aplenty
And sold for endless rue."
And I am two-and-twenty
And oh, 'tis true, 'tis true.

訣絕

我們再也不去那叢林，
那兒的月桂早已給斬盡了，
那草堂的頭上已脫掉
詩神常戴的桂冠；
年華在白日裡飛奔
一轉眼就要進黃昏；
那兒的月桂早已給斬盡了，
我們再也不去那叢林了

唉，我們再也不去，再也不去
那茂盛的樹林深處，
再也不去那月桂荒場，
不去那脫了桂冠的草堂。

一九五五年五月一日夜

We'll To The Woods No More

We'll to the woods no more,
The laurels are all cut,
The bowers are bare of bay
That once the Muses wore;
The year draws in the day
And soon will evening shut:
The laurels all are cut,
We'll to the woods no more.
Oh we'll no more, no more
To the leafy woods away,
To the high wild woods of laurel
And the bowers of bay no more.

最可愛的樹

樹木中最美麗的櫻桃，
枝頭正撲滿了花朵，
亭亭玉立在森林路旁
為暮春時節披著雪白的衣裳。

假如我能有七十年的光陰，
二十年早已代作了煙雲，
這七十減去二十，
只剩下五十個青春。

因為要欣賞繁花怒放的樹木，
五十個青春是過於短促，
所以我要前前後後走遍這森林路
去看這堆滿白雪的櫻桃樹。

一九五三年七月二十六日夜

Loveliest of Trees

Loveliest of trees,
The cherry now is hung with bloom along the bough,
And stands about the woodland ride
Wearing white for Eastertide.

Now, of my threescore years and ten,
Twenty will not come again,
And take from seventy springs a score,
It only leaves me fifty more.

And since to look at things in bloom
Fifty springs are little room,
About the woodlands I will go
To see the cherry hung with snow.

舊地

請給我一片綠葉滿枝的國土，
那兒叢生著樹木；

蕭蕭落木的地方就有悲傷；
我不愛沒有綠葉的地方。

唉，我出生的祖國
原是我心願長留的地方；
可是我不願的地方
我卻將永遠在那兒流亡。

我們記憶又遺忘，
都再也不曾尋到那舊地，
即使人們在深紅的網裡
從大海拖住夕陽。

一九五五年五月十九日夜十時

Give Me a Land of Boughs in Leaf

Give me a land of boughs in leaf,
A land of trees that stand;
Where trees are fallen there is grief;
I love no leafless land.

Alas, the country whence I fare,

It is where I would stay;

And where I would not, it is there

That I shall be for aye.

And one remembers and forgets

But 'tis not found again,

Not though they hale in crimsoned nets

The sunset from the main.

C・德・路易士（C. Day Lewis）

衝突

我歌唱著，像一個人在傾斜的
甲板上歌唱
來壯壯自己底膽子，雖然波濤壁立，
快要遮斷他底太陽。

像大鵝唱著歌，
向逆風投擲他們天然的答案，
不管是不是浪費了呼吸
或迎春到歡曲。

像海洋飛渡者躍上高空，
灑著最後的一滴精力，
即使前面還有陸地待爭取，
有工作待展翅。

去哦安靜的歌唱，
在雲的上面，場子外面，

因為在歌聲裡憂鬱會得到很快的釋放，
驕傲會得到平衡。

然而活在這兒，
像一個人活在兩種集中的權力夾縫中間，
中立救不了他，
職業也不愉快。

這些統統活不成：
那天真的翅膀馬上就會給射下來，
私有的星星也會凋落在血紅的黎明裡
那兒兩個世界正在鬥爭。

生命底紅色進展
感染到了驕傲，喚出人人底血，
把歌兒煉成一把刀鋒，
用悲哀製造深水炸彈。

於是在新的欲望下行動起來，
因為我們慣常建設和戀愛的地方
已成了無人之境，只有鬼魅能在
兩個火焰中間活下來。

一九五五年七月十日夜二時

The Conflict

I sang as one
Who on a tilting deck sings
To keep their courage up, thought the wave hangs
That shall cut off their sun.

As storm-cocks sing,
Flinging their natural answer in the wind's teeth,
And care not if it is waste of breath
Or birth-control of spring.

As ocean-flyer clings
To height, to the last drop of spirit driving on
While yet ahead is land to be won
And work for wings.

Singing I was at peace,
Above the clouds, outside the ring:
For sorrow finds a swift release in song
And pride in poise.

Yet living here,
As one between two massive powers I live

Whom neutrality cannot save
Nor occupation cheer.

None such shall be left alive:
The innocent wing is soon shot down,
And private stars fade in the blood-red dawn
Where two worlds strive.

The red advance of life
Contracts pride, calls out the common blood,
Beats song into a single-blade,
Makes a depth-charge of grief.

Move then with new desires,
For where we used to build and love
Is no man's land, and only ghosts can live
Between two fires.

E・E・卡明司（E. E. Cummings）

「甜蜜的春天是你的」

「甜蜜的春天是你底
我底時間是我們底
時間是因為春天的時間是戀愛的時間
富於活力的甜蜜的愛戀」

（快樂的小鳥
都飛翔在漂流在
歌唱的情緒裡
在百花齊開裡展翅）

愛人們來愛人們去
在閒蕩在追求
但每一對都絕對孤單
不見有旁人活著
（這樣的天空這樣的太陽
我從來沒見過也沒呼吸過
這麼多種的允諾）

沒有樹能數清它底葉
即使她自己一片片打開
但她千片萬片在閃光
只意味著一件驚心動魄的事情

（祕密地害羞地愛慕
輕輕地飛逸漂流
在開花中快活
永遠陶醉的自我在唱歌）

「甜蜜的春天是你底
我底時間是我們底
時間是因為春天的時間是戀愛的時間
富於活力的甜蜜的愛戀」

一九五七年元月二十日下午四時譯於20 Sumner Road, Cambridge, Mass

Sweet Spring

"Sweet spring is your
Time is my time is our
Time for springtime is lovetime
And viva sweet love"

(All the merry little birds are
Flying in the floating in the
Very spirits singing in
Are winging in the blossoming)

Lovers go and lovers come
Awandering awondering
But any two are perfectly
Alone there's nobody else alive

(Such a sky and such a sun
I never knew and neither breathed
Quite so many kinds of yes)

Not a tree can count his leaves
Each herself by opening
But shining who by thousands mean
Only one amazing thing

(Secretly adoring shyly
Tiny winging darting floating
Merry in the blossoming
Always joyful selves are singing)

"Sweet spring is your
Time is my time is our

Time for springtime is lovetime
And viva sweet love"

有些地方我從來沒遊過

有些地方我從來沒有遊過，樂於超出了
任何經驗之外，你底眼睛有它們底靜默：
在你最脆弱的姿態裡有些東西關閉我；
或我觸不到它們因為太近了

你輕輕的一瞥將容易把我打開
雖然我已關了自己像關緊我的手指
你說一瓣瓣打開我好像春天打開
（用巧妙地，神祕地接觸）她第一朵玫瑰

或者你如願意關了我，我和
我底生命就會非常美麗地突然關閉，
有如當此花之心幻想著
雪花到處小心飄落；

在這世間我們可能想像的一切都不及
你強烈的脆弱又力量：你這脆弱體

用牠萬國底色彩逼迫我，
交來了死，且永遠用每一呼吸

我不知你用什麼關閉和打開；
只在我內心裡就能瞭解
你眼睛的呼聲比所有的
玫瑰都深奧
沒有任何人，甚至連雨也沒有
這樣纖細的小手

一九五五年七月六日夜二時

Somewhere I Have Never Travelled

Somewhere I have never traveled, gladly beyond

Any experience, your eyes have their silence:

In your most frail gesture are things which enclose me,

Or which I cannot touch because they are too near

Your slightest look easily will unclose me

Though I have closed myself as fingers,

You open always petal by petal myself as Spring opens
(Touching skillfully, mysteriously) her first rose

Or if your wish be to close me, I and
My life will shut very beautifully, suddenly,
As when the heart of this flower imagines
The snow carefully everywhere descending;

Nothing which we are to perceive in this world equals
The power of your intense fragility: whose texture
Compels me with the color of its countries,
Rendering death and forever with each breathing

(I do not know what it is about you that closes
And opens; only something in me understands
The voice of your eyes is deeper than all roses)
Nobody, not even the rain, has such small hands

G・M・哈卜金斯
（Gerard Manley Hopkins）

圓滿癖

挑選出來的沉默，請為我唱，
請敲擊我螺旋形的耳鼓，
吹笛誘我到恬靜的牧場，
做我願聽得樂曲。

朱脣別用言語造形，
要可愛地瘖啞，像全盤封閉，
像來自一切降服之源的宵禁，
這只使你更會說嘴。

眼睛，快到漆黑的貝殼裡去睡眠，
尋找那尚未創生的光明：
你盯住的這一大堆一大捲
正會繞圈子，迷住人，逗眼睛。

口舌啊，你這味慾的孵育窩，
不可用美酒漂洗慾望。
罐頭盒該那麼甜，麵包皮該那麼鮮，
都要在神聖的齋戒裡來嘗。

鼻孔，你粗心的呼吸
須浪費騷擾，儲蓄驕傲，
香爐將噴出什麼風味
沿著那邊的神廟！

啊，撫摸合歡櫻草的手，
啊，收藏絲絨般草地的足，
你卻將走過那黃金街，
把造物者攘出又留宿。

還有貧窮呀，願你做新娘，
新婚的筵席早已開張，
水仙色的衣裳也已停當，
你底新郎卻不曾做不曾紡。

一九五六年十二月十七日夜

The Habit of Perfection

Elected Silence, sing to me
And beat upon my whorlèd ear,
Pipe me to pastures still and be
The music that I care to hear.

Shape nothing, lips; be lovely-dumb:
It is the shut, the curfew sent
From there where all surrenders come
Which only makes you eloquent.

Be shellèd, eyes, with double dark
And find the uncreated light:
This ruck and reel which you remark
Coils, keeps, and teases simple sight.

Palate, the hutch of tasty lust,
Desire not to be rinsed with wine:
The can must be so sweet, the crust
So fresh that come in fasts divine!

Nostrils, your careless breath that spend
Upon the stir and keep of pride,

What relish shall the censers send
Along the sanctuary side!

O feel-of-primrose hands, O feet
That want the yield of plushy sward,
But you shall walk the golden street
And you unhouse and house the Lord.

And, Poverty, be thou the bride
And now the marriage feast begun,
And lily-coloured clothes provide
Your spouse not laboured-at nor spun.

K・S・阿林（Kenneth Slade Alling）

獨自在公園的凳子上

在公園的凳子上那個他獨自
下棋，「一種純粹技術的玩藝。」
他散步在對角線的王國裡，
月亮底吸引力命令著他底步子，
只他獨個兒便把交通擁擠，但是
如果他下贏了自己
他也不會死，
只不過被放逐而已。

一九五五年六月四日夜十一時，與同居詩人Edwin van Boventer散步
歸來後譯。

　　譯注：原題作〈在公園的凳子上〉

On The Park Bench

On the park bench the man, alone,
Playing chess, "a game of pure skill."
He walks in a kingdom of diagonals
The moon's gravity orders his steps
The traffic is all of his own making, but
If he runs himself down
He won't die
He'll only be deported.

S・T・柯立芝
（Samuel Taylor Coleridge）

忽必烈漢

忽必烈漢在上都
下詔要建一座壯麗的圓頂快樂宮：
那兒聖潔的阿爾夫河
溜過深不可測的巖洞
流向沒有太陽的大海
把三十里肥沃的樂土
用高牆和城樓團團圍住：
花圈點綴著微波灩瀲的小河，
香樹開滿奇麗的花朵，
還有森林像山一般古老，
陽光下到處有綠葉的斑影環繞。

可是，啊，那陰深浪漫的石縫
歪裂在青山上，擎著一把翠柏！
真是一片蠻荒；神聖的，著了迷的，
直像在消瘦的月亮下

出沒著一個婦人在哭她的鬼戀！
不斷的混亂沸騰，石縫裡
地球急得心跳，喘氣，
直吐出一道粗大的噴泉，
斷斷續續，潑，潑，
巨大的水花跳著像彈回的冰雹，
也像打稻人連枷下粗糙的谷顆：
就在這舞躍的亂石裡
泉水老飛上那聖潔的河，
彎彎曲曲，一流就是十五里，
流過森林也流過山谷，
流進深不可測的巖洞，
浸到沒有生命的大海裡去：
就在這亂紛之中忽必烈聽見
遠遠地傳來祖先的聲音預告要大戰！

那圓頂歡樂之宮的影子
在波濤上浮到半路；
這兒聽得到變溶的調子
從噴泉和山洞裡流出
這奇跡啊是多麼稀少，
陽光照耀快樂宮伴著冰窖！

我忽然在幻影裡看見
一個姑娘拿了把銅絃琴：

她是個阿比西尼亞的少女，

她把琴兒輕彈，

唱著阿波雷山。

啊，我怎能在我心坎，

復活她的妙樂和清歌，

把我來挑逗得那麼深深地快樂，

請讓我用高亢而悠揚的音樂，

在空中築起那座圓頂宮，

那陽光燦爛的王宮！無數冰雪的巖洞！

凡是聽見了的人們都看得見牠們，

要齊聲大叫：當心！當心！

他那爍爍有光的眼睛，飄飄盪盪的頭髮！

請你織一條羅帶來纏他三圈，

恭恭敬敬閉了你的兩眼，

為的是他吃過甘露來，

還喝過樂園的奶。

一九五八年二月五日譯於哈佛

Xanadu—Kubla Khan[1]

In Xanadu did Kubla Khan

A stately pleasure-dome decree:

Where Alph, the sacred river, ran

Through caverns measureless to man

Down to a sunless sea.

So twice five miles of fertile ground

With walls and towers were girdled round:

And there were gardens bright with sinuous rills,

Where blossomed many an incense-bearing tree;

And here were forests ancient as the hills,

Enfolding sunny spots of greenery.

But oh! that deep romantic chasm which slanted

Down the green hill athwart a cedarn cover!

A savage place! as holy and enchanted

As e'er beneath a waning moon was haunted

By woman wailing for her demon-lover!

And from this chasm, with ceaseless turmoil seething,

As if this earth in fast thick pants were breathing,

A mighty fountain momently was forced:

Amid whose swift half-intermitted burst

---

[1] 【編者按】：此詩英文原文為編者所加，原書稿缺。

Huge fragments vaulted like rebounding hail,

Or chaffy grain beneath the thresher's flail:

And 'mid these dancing rocks at once and ever

It flung up momently the sacred river.

Five miles meandering with a mazy motion

Through wood and dale the sacred river ran,

Then reached the caverns measureless to man,

And sank in tumult to a lifeless ocean:

And 'mid this tumult Kubla heard from far

Ancestral voices prophesying war!

The shadow of the dome of pleasure

Floated midway on the waves;

Where was heard the mingled measure

From the fountain and the caves.

It was a miracle of rare device,

A sunny pleasure-dome with caves of ice!

A damsel with a dulcimer

In a vision once I saw:

It was an Abyssinian maid,

And on her dulcimer she played,

Singing of Mount Abora.

Could I revive within me

Her symphony and song,

To such a deep delight 'twould win me

That with music loud and long

I would build that dome in air,

That sunny dome! those caves of ice!

And all who heard should see them there,

And all should cry, Beware! Beware!

His flashing eyes, his floating hair!

Weave a circle round him thrice,

And close your eyes with holy dread,

For he on honey-dew hath fed

And drunk the milk of Paradise.

青年和老年

小詩，和花叢裡一陣恍蕩的微風，
像蜜蜂吸著希望當花蜜──
這兩樣本來都是我底！生命從滿了快樂，
伴著自然，希望，和詩歌，
當我還年輕的時光！

當我還年輕的時光？唉，可悲的「時光」！
於今和當時啊已是多麼兩樣！
這不是人手造成的住房，
這身這殼，於今把我虐待得好心傷，

在那懸空的高崖和閃爍的沙灘上
牠當時發出過多麼燦爛的光：
像美麗的小船不知來歷，
在曲折的湖泊與大海裡，
不靠帆兒也不靠槳，
也不怕風潮來顛盪！
這軀殼從來不憂慮天氣和風雨，
當青春和我還在那兒同住。

花可愛；愛情像花開；
友誼是遮蔭的大樹，
呀！友誼愛情和自由底愉快
落來像一陣驟雨，
只要我還沒有老去！

只要我還沒有老去？唉，這可悲的「還沒有」，
它告訴我青春已永去不留！
青春啊！在那內心多年甜蜜的光陰裡
誰也知道你我是二位一體，
說你已去了，那怎麼可能──
我該把這只當做一件好笑的掩飾！
你晚禱的鐘聲還沒曾敲過：──
你老是大膽地戴著假面具！
這偽裝是多麼奇怪可笑，
要騙我來相信你已經去了？

我看到這一絡絡的銀絲白髮，
這龍鍾的生態，和改變了的身材：
淚水還從你眼神裡放出光華！
青春和我還是同房。

露珠是早晨底寶石，
卻悵惘的黃昏底眼淚！
在沒有希望的地方，生命只是個警告，
它叫我們悲悼
當我們已經蒼老
──它老是用囉嗦的告別辭
只叫我們悲悼，
像個可憐的近親的客人
沒法兒無理地打發他走掉，
可是他早已在這兒呆得太久了，
卻還老在板著面孔開玩笑。

一九五六年十月譯於20 Sumner Road Cambridge, Mass

Youth And Age

Verse, a breeze 'mid blossoms straying,
Where Hope clung feeding, like a bee—

Both were mine! Life went a-maying
With Nature, Hope, and Poesy,
When I was young!

When I was young? —Ah, woeful When!
Ah! for the change 'twixt Now and Then!
This breathing house not built with hands,
This body that does me grievous wrong,
O'er aery cliffs and glittering sands
How lightly then it flashed along,
Like those trim skiffs, unknown of yore,
On winding lakes and rivers wide,
That ask no aid of sail or oar,
That fear no spite of wind or tide!
Nought cared this body for wind or weather
When Youth and I lived in't together.

Flowers are lovely; Love is flower-like;
Friendship is a sheltering tree;
O the joys! that came down shower-like,
Of Friendship, Love, and Liberty,
Ere I was old!

Ere I was old? Ah woeful Ere,
Which tells me, Youth's no longer here!

O Youth! for years so many and sweet
'Tis known that Thou and I were one,
I'll think it but a fond conceit—
It cannot be that Thou art gone!
Thy vesper-bell hath not yet tolled—
And thou wert aye a masker bold!
What strange disguise hast now put on,
To make believe that thou art gone?

I see these locks in silvery slips,
This drooping gait, this altered size:
But Springtide blossoms on thy lips,
And tears take sunshine from thine eyes:
Life is but Thought: so think I will
That Youth and I are housemates still.

Dew-drops are the gems of morning,
But the tears of mournful eve!
Where no hope is, life's a warning
That only serves to make us grieve
When we are old:
—That only serves to make us grieve
With oft and tedious taking-leave,
Like some poor nigh-related guest
That may not rudely be dismist;

Yet hath out-stayed his welcome while,

And tells the jest without the smile.

時間，真實和想象的
——一個寓言

在一個山頂曠原上

　（我原不知那是什麼地方，不過那本來是個幻境）

他們像鴕鳥的翅膀，展開成船帆，

兩個美麗的孩子在不斷地賽跑

妹妹和哥哥！

這個遠遠超過了那個；

可是她永遠跑著，頭卻向後看，

去看聽那後面的男孩：

因為，唉，他瞎了眼睛！

崎嶇和坦途他均走過了，

不知自己是在最前還是在最後。

Time, Real And Imaginary[2]

ON the wide level of a mountain's head
(I knew not where, but 'twas some faery place),
Their pinions, ostrich-like, for sails outspread,
Two lovely children run an endless race,
   A sister and a brother!
   This far outstripp'd the other;
   Yet ever runs she with reverted face,
   And looks and listens for the boy behind:
     For he, alas! is blind!
O'er rough and smooth with even step he pass'd,
And knows not whether he be first or last.

---

[2] 【編者按】：此詩英文原文為編者所加，原書稿缺。

W・H・台維斯
（W. H. Davies, 1870 - 1940）

月亮

你底美麗在我心靈彷徨，
你美麗的月亮啊，你這麼近這麼亮；
你底美麗使我像那個小孩一樣
哭著要你底光：
這小孩舉起一雙手膀
把你緊抱到她溫暖的胸膛。

雖然今夜有無數的鳥兒唱歌
但他們底歌喉被你銀白的光輝透過；
讓我深沉的靜默替我訴說
比他們甜蜜的調子替他們訴說的還多：
那崇拜你到連音樂也無法表達了的人
是比你底夜鶯偉大得多。

一九五三年七月二十二日夜

The Moon

Thy beauty haunts me heart and soul,
O thou fair moon,so close and bright;
Thy beauty makes me like the child
That cries aloud to own thy light:
The little child that lifts each arm
To press thee to her bosom warm.

Though there are birds that sing this night
With thy white beams across their throats,
Let my deep silence speak for me
More than for them their sweetest notes:
Who worships thee till music fails
Is greater than nightingales.

野心

我曾有過野心，
使天使們墮落的就是這罪行；

主啊，我一步一步爬上去，
爬上了「地獄」。

如今我回復了平靜，
還變得更聰明，
主啊，讓我底墮落和下降，
是降落到「天堂」。

一九五三年七月二十二日夜

Ambition

I had Ambition, by which sin
The angels fell;
I climbed and, step by step, O Lord,
Ascended into Hell.
Returning now to peace and quiet,
And made more wise,
Let my descent and fall, O Lord,
Be into Paradise.

散學了

女孩笑，
男孩鬧；
狗汪汪，
散學了。

貓兒跑，
馬兒奔；
鳥兒飛，
進樹林。

寶寶醒，
眼睛開；
叫化了
藏起來。
老頭兒
顛回家；
孩子們
歡迎來！

一九五三年七月二十四日夜

School's Out

Girls scream,
Boys shout;
Dogs bark,
Schools out.

Cats run,
Horses shy;
Into trees
Birds fly.

Babes wake
Open-eyed;
If they can,
Tramps hide.

Old man,
Hobble home;
Merry mites,
Welcome.

最好的朋友

現在我該坐車，
還是該步行？
享樂說：「坐車」；
愉快答道：「步行」。

現在我該怎麼樣，
流浪呢還是在家？
享樂說：「流浪」；
愉快卻說：「在家」。

現在我該跳舞，
還是該坐著做夢？
愉快答道：「坐著吧」；
享樂卻叫道：「跳舞」。

你們兩位
誰是更可親？
享樂曾甜蜜地媚笑，
可是愉快卻和我接過吻。

一九五三年七月二十四日

The Best Friend

Now shall I walk
Or shall I ride?
"Ride", Pleasure said;
"Walk", Joy replied.

Now what shall I —
Stay home or roam?
"Roam", Pleasure said;
And Joy – "stay home."

Now shall I dance,
Or sit for dreams?
"Sit," answers Joy;
"Dance," Pleasure screams.

Which of ye two
Will kindest be?
Pleasure laughed sweet,
But Joy kissed me.

給一個女朋友[1]

既然你已變卦
那你就說真話：
我們是人們常把讚美
獻給任何石頭或野草，
獻給那在淒風裡
生氣的啞巴鳥；
獻給這個，那個，或者你——
只要是第一次碰上的東西。

我恰好第一次碰上了你，
當我血液裡的生命力——
從沒人知道的地方來到——
正達到了最高潮；
這時候無論任何東西，
舊的也好，新的也好，
都能夠把我底詩引起——
不管是棍子，骨頭，爛布，或者你。

一九五三年七月二十二日夜深

---

[1] 【編者按】：原稿缺此詩英文原文。

閒暇

這人生將變成怎麼樣，若是我們滿懷憂傷，
沒功夫閒蕩。

沒功夫都留在樹枝下眺望，
自在得像牛羊。

若是經過樹林時，沒功夫去望一望
松鼠在草裡把堅果藏在什麼地方。

白天裡，也沒有閒時
去看看那像靜夜的天空般盛滿著星星的流水。

連「美」底一閃眼也沒功夫去回顧
和注視她底腳步兒怎麼跳舞。

沒功夫等到她底嘴角兒來點綴那一笑，
那一笑她早就用眼睛開始了。

這人生會多麼無味，若是我們滿懷憂傷，
沒功夫閒蕩。

一九五三年七月二十二日下午

Leisure

What is this life if, full of care,
We have no time to stand and stare.
No time to stand beneath the boughs
And stare as long as sheep or cows.
No time to see, when woods we pass,
Where squirrels hide their nuts in grass.
No time to see, in broad daylight,
Streams full of stars, like skies at night.
No time to turn at Beauty's glance,
And watch her feet, how they can dance.
No time to wait till her mouth can
Enrich that smile her eyes began.
A poor life this if, full of care,
We have no time to stand and stare.

榜樣

這兒有一隻蝴蝶
是一個好榜樣；

牠伏在一塊粗硬的崖石上，
卻依然快活；
在那毫無芳香的石頭上
牠沒有伴侶，孤單而寂寞。

現在讓我底床也那麼粗硬，
我一點也不耽心；
我要想這隻小蝴蝶
一樣的
牠愉快地心情有一種魔法
把石頭變成花。

　　W・H・台維斯是「一個真正天真的人，把零零星星的事物寫
成零零星星的詩。」——蕭伯納：一個超級流浪者底自傳序。

一九五三年七月二十二日下午

The Example

Here's an example from
A Butterfly;
That on a rough, hard rock

Happy can lie;
Friendless and all alone
On this unsweetened stone.

Now let my bed be hard
No care take I;
I'll make my joy like this
Small Butterfly;
Whose happy heart has power
To make a stone a flower.

W・H・敖敦（W. H. Auden）

可是我不能

時間只會說：我早告訴過你了；
時間只知道我們不能不付出的代價；
要是我能告訴你，我會讓你知道。

要是丑角們表演時我們應該哭，
要是音樂家演奏是我們應該跑跳，
時間只會說：我早告訴過你了。

可是這兒沒有命運可以預告，
因為我愛你過於我所能說的，
要是我能告訴你，我會讓你知道。

風兒吹時一定有個來的地方，
葉兒一定有些理由才枯凋；
時間只會說：我早告訴過你了。
也許玫瑰真的要生長，

幻想認真地打算留著；
要是我能告訴你，我會讓你知道。

假如獅子能站起來要走開，
而一切的小河與兵士都要逃跑；
難道時間只會說我早告訴過你了？
要是我能告訴你，我會讓你知道。

一九五三年七月十四日

But I Can't

Time will say nothing but I told you so,
Time only knows the price we have to pay;
If I could tell you I would let you know.

If we should weep when clowns put on their show,
If we should stumble when musicians play,
Time will say nothing but I told you so.

There are no fortunes to be told, although,
Because I love you more than I can say,
If I could tell you I would let you know.

The winds must come from somewhere when they blow,
There must be reasons why the leaves decay;
Time will say nothing but I told you so.

Perhaps the roses really want to grow,
The vision seriously intends to stay;
If I could tell you I would let you know.

Suppose the lions all get up and go,
And the brooks and soldiers run away;
Will Time say nothing but I told you so?
If I could tell you I would let you know.

法律就像愛情

園丁們說，法律就是太陽，
法律是一切園丁們
明天，昨天，今天
都服從的太陽。
法律是老人們底智慧，
衰弱的祖父們高聲責備；
孫子們發出尖銳的聲音，
法律是青年人底精神。

牧師用傳教的姿態說，
法律對不便於傳教的民族講解，
法律就是我傳教書本裡的話句，
就是我底教堂和傳教的講台。

法官向鼻梁下一瞧，
清楚而極嚴厲地說道，
法律就是我早告訴過你的那一套，
法律是我以為你已知道了的那一套，
法律只是讓我再來對你說明一句，
法律就是「這個法律」。

可是那守法的學者們卻寫道：
法律既不錯也不對，
法律知識受了時代和環境懲罰的一些犯罪，
法律就是人們隨時隨地穿著的衣服，
法律就是早安和晚安這些招呼。

別的人們說，法律是我們底命運；
別的人們說，法律是我們底國家；
別的人們說，別的人們說
法律已沒有了，
法律早走了。

還有那喧鬧憤怒的群眾
老是非常憤怒和喧鬧地說，

法律就是「我們」，
而那溫柔的白痴卻老是溫柔地說，
法律就是「我」。

哎呦，要是我們知道
我們對法律知道得比他們並不多；
要是我也和你一樣
除了大家都同意
高興地或難過地同意
法律是怎麼回事
而且大家都知道這麼回事
除了這，我就和你差不多
只知道什麼該做什麼不該做；
要是，因為想到了
把法律和別的字看成相同是荒謬
所以我不能和那麼多的人相似
再說法律是怎麼回事；
那末，我們和他們也就一樣
不能禁止這普通的願意猜想，
也不能溜出我們自己底崗位
跑進一個不相干的境地。

我雖然至少能夠
把你和我底空虛
約束到只膽怯地說出

一種膽怯的類似，
我們說還可以誇張：
我說法律就和愛情相像。

像愛情我們不知道它到底所在和原因
像愛情我們不能強迫或逃避
像愛情我們時常哭它
像愛情我們很少堅持它。

一九五三年七月五日夜

Law, Say the Gardeners, Is the Sun

Law, say the gardeners, is the sun,
Law is the one
All gardeners obey
To-morrow, yesterday, to-day.

Law is the wisdom of the old,
The impotent grandfathers shrilly scold;
The grandchildren put out a treble tongue,
Law is the senses of the young.

Law, says the priest with a priestly look,

Expounding to an unpriestly people,

Law is the words in my priestly book,

Law is my pulpit and my steeple.

Law, says the judge as he looks down his nose,

Speaking clearly and most severely,

Law is as I've told you before,

Law is as you know I suppose,

Law is but let me explain it once more,

Law is The Law.

Yet law-abiding scholars write:

Law is neither wrong nor right,

Law is only crimes

Punished by places and by times,

Law is the clothes men wear

Anytime, anywhere,

Law is Good morning and Good night.

Others say, Law is our Fate;

Others say, Law is our State;

Others say, others say

Law is no more,

Law has gone away.

And always the loud angry crowd,

Very angry and very loud,

Law is We,

And always the soft idiot softly Me.

If we, dear, know we know no more

Than they about the Law,

If I no more than you

Know what we should and should not do

Except that all agree

Gladly or miserably

That the Law is

And that all know this

If therefore thinking it absurd

To identify Law with some other word,

Unlike so many men

I cannot say Law is again,

No more than they can we suppress

The universal wish to guess

Or slip out of our own position

Into an unconcerned condition.

Although I can at least confine

Your vanity and mine

To stating timidly

A timid similarity,
We shall boast anyway:
Like love I say.

Like love we don't know where or why,
Like love we can't compel or fly,
Like love we often weep,
Like love we seldom keep.

停了一切的鐘錶

停了一切的鐘錶，把電話拆掉，
用油膩的骨頭逗著狗兒莫叫，
停奏鋼琴，鼓息了，抬出棺材，
讓哭喪的人們到來。

讓飛機盤旋在頭上慘叫，
在天空塗寫下惡耗：「他死了。」
把皺紗的結兒圍在野鴿底白頸上，
叫交通警察戴上黑色的棉手套。

他本來是我底南，北，東，西，
是我底工作周，和禮拜天的休息，

是我底中午，半夜，歌唱，和談笑；
我滿以為愛情會永存：我錯了。

現在不需要星星；快把每顆都熄了：
包紮起月亮，拆毀掉太陽；
把海洋傾倒，把森林掃蕩；
因為如今再也沒有一點兒好處了。

一九五三年七月四日夜

Song: Stop All The Clocks

Stop all the clocks, cut off the telephone,
Prevent the dog from barking with a juicy bone,
Silence the pianos and with muffled drum
Bring out the coffin, let the mourners come.
Let aeroplanes circle moaning overhead
Scribbling on the sky the message He Is Dead,
Put crepe bows round the white necks of the public doves,
Let the traffic policemen wear black cotton gloves.

He was my North, my South, my East and West,
My working week and my Sunday rest,

My noon, my midnight, my talk, my song;

I thought that love would last for ever: I was wrong.

The stars are not wanted now: put out every one;

Pack up the moon and dismantle the sun;

Pour away the ocean and sweep up the wood.

For nothing now can ever come to any good.

卡爾‧山德堡（Carl Sandburg）

小草

在奧斯特立茲[1]戰場和滑鐵盧把屍首堆高。
把他們剷掉讓我來工作──
我是小草咯；我掩埋一切。

也在蓋地斯堡把屍首堆高。
還在伊卜爾[2]和阜潭[3]戰地把屍首堆高。
把他們剷掉讓我來工作。
兩年了，十年了，過路的人向司機問道：
這是什麼地方？
我們到了那裡了？

---

[1] Austerlitz是捷克中部小鎮，一八〇五年拿破侖在這兒擊敗俄奧洲軍。
[2] Ypres是比利時西部小鎮，第一次世界大戰時這兒有多次血戰。
[3] Verdun是法國東部的碉堡城市。一九一六年第一次世界大戰時法國人在這兒一次
    最兇惡的戰役中阻遇了德軍的進攻。

我是小草。

讓我工作。

一九五五年六月二十五日夜二時

Grass

Pile the bodies high at Austerlitz and Waterloo,

Shovel them under and let me work—

I am the grass; I cover all.

And pile them high at Gettysburg

And pile them high at Ypres and Verdun.

Shovel them under and let me work.

Two years, ten years, and passengers ask the conductor:

What place is this?

Where are we now?

I am the grass.

Let me work.

白朗寧（Robert Browing）

終身的愛

1

跑了一間房又一間房，

我找遍了這座屋子，

我們住在一起

心啊，一點也別怕，因為心，你會找到她，

下次，會找到她本人！不是她說留下來的

簾內的煩惱，床上的芳香！

那壁上的花說，經她拂拭後曾重新開放。

2

但是日子消磨了

還是一條門有一條門；

我永遠摸索的命運──

從廂房到正廳，找遍了這大廈。

老是這麼個緣法！我進來時她偏出去了

我尋了一整天，──別管吧！

可是你知道，天快黑啦，──還有那麼多的房間要探查，
那麼多的私屋要找，那麼毒的房要纏夾！

一九五七年二月十七日下午五時半

Love in a Life

Room after room,

I hunt the house through

We inhabit together.

Heart, fear nothing, for, heart, thou shalt find her,

Next time, herself!—not the trouble behind her

Left in the curtain, the couch's perfume!

As she brushed it, the cornice-wreath blossomed anew,—

Yon looking-glass gleamed at the wave of her feather.

Yet the day wears,

And door succeeds door;

I try the fresh fortune—

Range the wide house from the wing to the centre.

Still the same chance! she goes out as I enter.

Spend my whole day in the quest,—who cares?

But 'tis twilight, you see,—with such suites to explore,

Such closets to search, such alcoves to importune!

白朗寧夫人
（Elizabeth Barrett Browning）

白朗寧夫人底情詩

14

你若要愛我，請不要為了別的，
除非只為了愛情，你不要說道：
「我愛她是為了她底笑，為了她底容貌，
為了她溫柔的傾訴，為了她巧妙的
心思和我底很合得好，為了在這日子裡
戀愛一定會帶來快樂的安寧不少。」——
因為，親愛的，這些東西的本身都不可靠，
有時為了你，它們也會變卦——這樣造成的
愛情也可以這樣毀掉，你愛我也別為了
只是要用你親切的憐恤來揩幹我底臉——
因為老是受著你底安慰，我也許會忘掉
哭泣，那時就將失去你底愛憐！
請你愛我只為了愛情，這樣，通過了
愛情底永恆，你就會把我永遠愛憐。

35

假如我把一切都交給你，
你願不願意交換，也把一切交給我？
我能否把家庭的蜜語和祝福都不錯過？
把每次交互的甜吻都不放棄？
若是我走到一座金碧輝煌的新廳裡，
望見了另一個家，我也不會驚異麼？
不，你可願把我放在那地方藏著？
那兒充滿了毫絲知覺的眼睛，不知變幻是怎麼回事。
這該是最難的了，萬事都會證明
要征服憂鬱，比要征服愛情更不容易。
因為憂鬱實在是愛情和憂鬱的相並。
唉，我憂鬱過所以很難愛了。但是
你愛我吧──你願意麼？請打開你底心，
收藏在你鴿鳥底溼翅膀裡。

43

我是怎樣愛你？讓我來算算看：
我愛你愛到我靈魂能到達的高深和廣寬，
當它銷聲匿跡，去的那麼遙遠，

去把萬有底極限和理想的美追探。
我對著太陽也對著燭光底燦爛
起誓，愛你像每天最必需的安恬。
我自由地愛你，像人們在爭取人權；

我純潔地愛你，像人們避免稱讚。

我用我往日憂愁中的激情

和童年時的信心來愛你。

我用我失去聖徒時失去的愛情

來愛你──我用我整個生命底呼吸，

笑容，和眼淚來愛你！──並且，上帝如果命令，

我將只有在死後更好好地愛你。

一九五七年二月十六日下午四時半譯於Cambridge

Sonnets from the Portuguese[1]

14

If thou must love me, let it be for nought

Except for love's sake only. Do not say

I love her for her smile ... her look ... her way

Of speaking gently, ... for a trick of thought

That falls in well with mine, and certes brought

A sense of pleasant ease on such a day'—

For these things in themselves, Belovèd, may

---

[1] 【編者按】：此詩英文原文為編者所加，原書稿缺。

Be changed, or change for thee,—and love, so wrought,

May be unwrought so. Neither love me for

Thine own dear pity's wiping my cheeks dry,—

A creature might forget to weep, who bore

Thy comfort long, and lose thy love thereby!

But love me for love's sake, that evermore

Thou may'st love on, through love's eternity.

35

If I leave all for thee, wilt thou exchange

And be all to me? Shall I never miss

Home-talk and blessing and the common kiss

That comes to each in turn, nor count it strange,

When I look up, to drop on a new range

Of walls and floors ... another home than this?

Nay, wilt thou fill that place by me which is

Filled by dead eyes too tender to know change?

That's hardest. If to conquer love, has tried,

To conquer grief, tries more ... as all things prove;

For grief indeed is love and grief beside.

Alas, I have grieved so I am hard to love.

Yet love me—wilt thou? Open thine heart wide,

And fold within, the wet wings of thy dove.

43

How do I love thee? Let me count the ways.

I love thee to the depth and breadth and height

My soul can reach, when feeling out of sight

For the ends of being and ideal grace.

I love thee to the level of every day's

Most quiet need, by sun and candle-light.

I love thee freely, as men strive for right;

I love thee purely, as they turn from praise.

I love thee with the passion put to use

In my old griefs, and with my childhood's faith.

I love thee with a love I seemed to lose

With my lost saints. I love thee with the breath,

Smiles, tears, of all my life; and, if God choose,

I shall but love thee better after death.

白墨安特（William Cullen Bryant）

我解除了這蠱惑了我許久的符咒

我解除了這蠱惑了我許久的符咒，
這親愛的，親愛的詩魔。
我說過，這詩人懶惰的藝術
再也不會來把我底壯年消磨，
因為詩歌雖然生來就非常美麗，
卻老是與貧窮和輕蔑相結合。

我把這符咒解除了──
它底魔力連一分鐘也不能再束縛我了。
可是啊，這實在太輕率了！
我怎能忘記它底誘惑力還在我底周遭？
就在這時候，我到處一瞧，
到處充滿了大自然永恆的微笑。

依舊流連在我眼前的
是那繁華和流水底光明，

是那星星和太陽底光榮，——
這些和詩歌原是一體。
當我在塵世還沒有老去之前，
它們又使我憶起了對這詩歌的愛戀。

一九五三年六月三日下午譯於密大圖

I Broke the Spell That Held Me Long

I broke the spell that held me long,

The dear, dear witchery of song.

I said, the poet's idle lore

Shall waste my prime of years no more,

For Poetry, though heavenly born,

Consorts with poverty and scorn.

I broke the spell—nor deemed its power

Could fetter me another hour.

Ah, thoughtless! how could I forget

Its causes were around me yet?

For wheresoe'er I looked, the while,

Was Nature's everlasting smile.

Still came and lingered on my sight

Of flowers and streams the bloom and light,

And glory of the stars and sun;—

And these and poetry are one.

They, ere the world had held me long,

Recalled me to the love of song.

色爾薇亞‧卜萊芝（Sylvia Plath）

比喻

我是個九個音節的謎語，

一頭象，一座笨重的房子，

一隻站在兩條瓜蔓上漫步的西瓜。

啊，生果，象牙，文本！

這捲大麵色發酵而膨脹。

這肥大的綠色裡綠是新鑄的。

我是個方法，一座舞台，一頭幼年的母牛

我吃過一袋綠蘋果，

搭上了列車，再也下不來。

一九八七年六月一日

Metaphors[1]

I'm a riddle in nine syllables,

An elephant, a ponderous house,

A melon strolling on two tendrils.

O red fruit, ivory, fine timbers!

This loaf's big with its yeasty rising.

Money's new-minted in this fat purse.

I'm a means, a stage, a cow in calf.

I've eaten a bag of green apples,

Boarded the train there's no getting off.

---

[1] 【編者按】：此詩英文原文為編者所加，原書稿缺。

艾莉諾・魏勒（Elinor Wylie）

什麼地方，啊，什麼地方？

我不必為了要離你那麼遙遠而死去，
使你不能發現
我逃避，隱居的地方，
和我底足跡
是寫在血上或是在露水上；
我只要瞞住你
把我底足跡隱藏在
遺落的羊齒樹種子裡
或者在柔軟的霜片裡。
牠們會浮到空中，浸在水底，
走進星叢，埋在土裡，
或者在隔壁房屋的
頂樓上，地窖裡；
你就再也看不見我了，

雖然我夜夜躲藏
在你底床上，在你底身旁。

一九五三年七月二十四日

Where, O, Where?

I need not die to go so far
You cannot know my escape, my retreat,
And the prints of my feet
Written in blood or dew;
They shall be hid from you,
In fern-seed lost or the soft flakes of frost.
They will turn somewhere under water,
Over air, to earth space or stellar,
Or the garret or the cellar
Of the house next door,
You shall see me no more
though each night I hide in your bed,
At your side.

天鵝絨的鞋子

讓我們在白雪裡散步
在無聲的地方；
用悠閒的腳步
恬靜地踱著
在白色花邊的披面紗下。

我要穿上絲鞋，
你要穿上毛鞋，
像白牛底奶一樣白，
比海鷗底胸脯
還要嫵媚。

我們要在風的平靜裡
走過那悄悄的街市；
我們要踏在白色的乳毛上，
踏在銀色羊毛上，
踏在更柔軟的東西上。

我們要穿上天鵝絨的鞋子散步：
無論到什麼地方
靜寂會像露水般落下來
落在下面白色的寂靜上。
我們去雪上散步。

魏勒發表她第一本代表詩集《補風網》時已經三十六歲了。這詩集裡的作品清脆卻真實；有水晶般的透明，也有水晶般的冷雋，牠像這女詩人自己，挑剔而微妙。從技巧上說，牠不失為輝煌，從來沒有詩歌能像「天鵝絨的鞋子」這詩把冬天底境界和雪中底靜默描繪得這麼巧妙的。

一九五三年七月二十四日

Velvet Shoes

Let us walk in the white snow
In a soundless space;
With footsteps quiet and slow,
At a tranquil pace,
Under veils of white lace.

I shall go shod in silk,
And you in wool,
White as white cow's milk,
More beautiful
Than the breast of a gull.

We shall walk through the still town
In a windless peace;
We shall step upon white down,
Upon silver fleece,
Upon softer than these.

We shall walk in velvet shoes:
Wherever we go
Silence will fall like dews
On white silence below.
We shall walk in the snow.

Elinor Wylie was thirty-six before Nets to Catch The Wind, her first representative book of poems, appeared. The verse was delicate but firm; it had the clarity as well as the coldness of crystal. It was, like the woman herself, fastidious and subtle. Technically it was seldom less than brilliant; never has the texture of a winter day, the very silence of snow, been so skillfully communicated as in "Velvet Shoes."—Louis Untermeyer

艾德格・坡（Edgar Allan Poe）

海市

看！死神在陌生而荒涼的城廓
替自己造了個王座，
遠在那暗淡的西方，
信男善女和窮凶極惡
早已走向了永恆的安息。
那兒的神殿，王室，和樓閣
（不搖抖的古閣！）
和我們的完全不同。
對著突為其來的旋風，
在天空下服服帖帖地
海水躺著發愁。

神聖的天空沒有一絲光線投射
向這海市的慢慢長夜；
但從那蒼白的海外
光明靜悄悄地照上那樓台——

照耀在那遠遠的自由的塔尖——
照在穹窿屋頂——螺旋屋頂——威嚴的宮殿——
照在寺院上——和巴比倫式的高牆——
照在蔭蔽的久已荒廢的草堂
那兒雕鏤著寶石花和常青藤——
照到無數的稀奇的古跡名勝
那壁上纏結著迂回的花蔓，
薜荔，青菫，和紫羅蘭。
在天空下服服帖帖地
海水躺著發愁。
那兒的塔尖和影子是多麼混沌
好像在空中搖擺不定，
當死神從這城市傲慢的樓上
巨人般向下面眺望。

那裡裂著嘴巴的墳墓和開敞的寺院
與閃爍的波濤一齊打著呵欠；
但財寶並不藏在
每個偶像的鑽石的眼珠裡——

並非珠光寶氣的死人
掀起了水上的風波；
因為，唉！在這荒涼的平鏡上
每一絲波紋蕩漾——
沒有潮水來報告

遙遠的愉快些的海洋要起風——
沒有波紋暗示著
這未死的海上已經起了風。

可是看，空中有了騷動！
波濤——波濤忽然在發抖！
樓閣好像慢慢下沉
把暗潮擠得向一邊滾——
樓頂像是在薄膜的天空裡
無力地造成了個真空
這時波濤的紅光更紅——
時光衰弱地喘息——
當塵世沒有呻吟，
那海市從此快沉沒又沉沒時，
地獄從千百座王位上升起，
要給它華嚴的意境。

一九五八年元月二十一日譯於哈佛

The City in the Sea[1]

Lo! Death has reared himself a throne

In a strange city lying alone

Far down within the dim West,

Where the good and the bad and the worst and the best

Have gone to their eternal rest.

There shrines and palaces and towers

(Time-eaten towers that tremble not!)

Resemble nothing that is ours.

Around, by lifting winds forgot,

Resignedly beneath the sky

The melancholy waters lie.

No rays from the holy heaven come down

On the long night-time of that town;

But light from out the lurid sea

Streams up the turrets silently-

Gleams up the pinnacles far and free-

Up domes- up spires- up kingly halls-

Up fanes- up Babylon-like walls-

Up shadowy long-forgotten bowers

Of sculptured ivy and stone flowers-

---

[1]　【編者按】：此詩英文原文為編者所加，原書稿缺。

Up many and many a marvellous shrine

Whose wreathed friezes intertwine

The viol, the violet, and the vine.

Resignedly beneath the sky

The melancholy waters lie.

So blend the turrets and shadows there

That all seem pendulous in air,

While from a proud tower in the town

Death looks gigantically down.

There open fanes and gaping graves

Yawn level with the luminous waves;

But not the riches there that lie

In each idol's diamond eye-

Not the gaily-jewelled dead

Tempt the waters from their bed;

For no ripples curl, alas!

Along that wilderness of glass-

No swellings tell that winds may be

Upon some far-off happier sea-

No heavings hint that winds have been

On seas less hideously serene.

But lo, a stir is in the air!

The wave- there is a movement there!

As if the towers had thrust aside,

In slightly sinking, the dull tide-

As if their tops had feebly given

A void within the filmy Heaven.

The waves have now a redder glow-

The hours are breathing faint and low-

And when, amid no earthly moans,

Down, down that town shall settle hence,

Hell, rising from a thousand thrones,

Shall do it reverence.

艾默生（Ralph Waldo Emerson）

豪氣

紅酒喝醉了流氓，
白糖把奴才吃胖，
玫瑰和籐葉給小丑打扮；
宙士卻用雷雲做綵冠，
時常掛著威嚴底花圈，
用閃電在頭上接纏；
英雄不是糖果所餵成，
他每天吃著自己底心；
監獄就是偉人們底睡房，
逆風正是為了順水推航。

一九五三年六月二十七日下午

Heroism

Ruby wine is drunk by knaves

Sugar spends to fatten slaves,

Rose and vine-leaf deck buffoons;

Thunderclouds are Jove's festoons,

Drooping oft in wreaths of dread

Lightning-knotted round his head;

The hero is not fed on sweets,

Daily his own heart he eats;

Chambers of the great are jails,

And head-winds right for royal sails.

亨利・朗法羅
（Henry Wadsworth Longfellow）

潮漲又潮平

潮漲又潮平。
黃昏潏鷸鳴；
海灘沙暗濕，
旅客趣市行。
潮漲又潮平。

暮靄侵牆屋，
海嘯喚黃昏；
微波柔素手，
揩沙沒足痕。
潮漲又潮平。

平明馬嘶廄，
僕禦呼喚聲；
白日復歸來，

不復見行人。
潮漲又潮平。

一九五七年十二月一日夜九時至九時一刻

The tide rises, the tide falls,[1]

The tide rises, the tide falls,
The twilight darkens, the curlew calls;
Along the sea-sands damp and brown
The traveller hastens toward the town,
    And the tide rises, the tide falls.

Darkness settles on roofs and walls,
But the sea, the sea in the darkness calls;
The little waves, with their soft, white hands,
Efface the footprints in the sands,
    And the tide rises, the tide falls.

---

[1] 【編者按】：此詩英文原文為編者所加，原書稿缺。

The morning breaks; the steeds in their stalls

Stamp and neigh, as the hostler calls;

The day returns, but nevermore

Returns the traveller to the shore,

And the tide rises, the tide falls.

克蕾司丁娜・羅色蒂
（ **Christina Rossetti** ）

我死後

我最親愛的啊，我死後
別為我唱悲傷的歌；
你別種玫瑰在我頭上，
也莫種陰森的翠柏：
好讓我墳上的青草
給驟雨和露珠來滴溼；
要是你情願，就記念吧，
要是你情願，就忘記吧。

我不會看見那陰影，
我不會感覺那雨；
我不會聽到那隻夜鶯
歌唱，牠像有無限的痛苦；
在不明不安的黃昏裡
我和夢兒沉醉，

也許我會記憶，
也許我會忘記。

一九五五年六月二十四日下午二時

When I Am Dead, My Dearest

When I am dead, my dearest,
Sing no sad songs for me;
Plant thou no roses at my head,
Nor shady cypress tree:
Be the green grass above me
With showers and dewdrops wet;
And if thou wilt, remember,
And if thou wilt, forget.

I shall not see the shadows,
I shall not feel the rain;
I shall not hear the nightingale
Sing on, as if in pain:
And dreaming through the twilight
That doth not rise nor set,

Haply I may remember,
And haply may forget.

附錄：歌

冠列士丁娜・羅塞華作、徐志摩譯

我死了的時候，親愛的，
別為我唱悲傷的歌；
我墳上不必安插薔薇，
也無需遮蔭的柏樹：
讓蓋著我的青青的草
淋著雨，也沾著露珠；
假如你願意，請記著我，
要是你甘心，忘了我。

我在不見地面的青蔭，
覺不到雨露的甜蜜；
再聽不見夜鶯的歌喉
在黑夜裡傾吐悲啼；
在悠久的昏暮中迷惘，
陽光不升起，也不消翳；

我也許，也許我記得你，
我也許，我也許忘記。

《新月》，第一卷第四號，一九二八年六月十日，「詩」，頁四。

狄朗・湯瑪司（Dylan Thomas）

不要輕輕走進那訣別的良夜

不要輕輕走進那訣別的良夜，
在日子的末了，老年應該燃燒和狂嘯；
憤怒，憤怒反抗者光的死滅。

雖然智者臨終時知道黑暗是多麼正確，
因為他們的語言還沒有岔射出閃電，他們倒
不要輕輕走進那訣別的良夜。

好人最後一揮手，叫聲他們脆弱的功業
也許原該在綠色的海灣草原上快活舞蹈，
憤怒，憤怒反抗這光的死滅。
野人本來瞥見太陽飛奔就歌唱歡躍，
來不及瞭解，他們就隨著它的消失而悲悼，
不要輕輕走進那訣別的良夜。

嚴肅的人接近死亡時用刺人目盲的眼光觀測
盲目本來可能像流星吐焰，快樂陶陶，
憤怒，憤怒反抗這光的死滅。

而你，我底父親，在那悲哀的巔峰，今夜
請用你猛烈的眼淚來詛咒、祝福我，我禱告。
不要輕輕走進那訣別的良夜。
憤怒，憤怒反抗這光的死滅。

一九八九年九月十五日清晨三時

Do Not Go Gentle into That Good Night

Do not go gentle into that good night,
Old age should burn and rage at close of day;
Rage, rage against the dying of the light.
Though wise men at their end know dark is right,
Because their words had forked no lightning they
Do not go gentle into that good night.

Good men, the last wave by, crying how bright
Their frail deeds might have danced in a green bay,
Rage, rage against the dying of the light.

Wild men who caught and sang the sun in flight,
And learn, too late, they grieved it on its way,
Do not go gentle into that good night.

Grave men, near death, who see with blinding sight
Blind eyes could blaze like meteors and be gay,
Rage, rage against the dying of the light.

And you, my father, there on the sad height,
Curse, bless me now with your fierce tears, I pray.
Do not go gentle into that good night.
Rage, rage against the dying of the light.

貝多斯（Thomas Lovell Beddoes）

要是有夢賣

要是有夢賣，
你要買什麼夢？
有些只值一隻串鈴，
有些只值輕輕的歎息一聲，
這一歎，從生命底新冠
只搖落玫瑰花葉一片。
要是有夢賣，
能夠預告悲歡，
當叫賣的人把串鈴搖動，
你要買什麼夢？

一個寂靜的山村，
草堂就在鄰近，
綠蔭蔥蘢，使我底憂心平靜，
在那兒終老餘生。
這般生命新冠上的珠寶，

我情願為牠而傾倒。

如果願有什麼夢就有什麼夢，

只這個夢最能把我底病醫好，

我正要買這個夢。

一九五五年六月十八日下午去尼加拉大瀑布路上

If There Were Dreams To Sell

If there were dreams to sell,

What would you buy?

Some cost a passing bell;

Some a light sigh,

That shakes from Life's fresh crown

Only a rose-leaf down.

If there were dreams to sell,

Merry and sad to tell,

And the crier rang the bell,

What would you buy?

A cottage lone and still,

With bowers nigh,

Shadowy, my woes to still,

Until I die.

Such pearl from Life's fresh crown

Fain would I shake me down.

Were dreams to have at will,

This best would heal my ill,

This would I buy.

拉伏勒斯（Richard Lovelace）

赴戰
——給露卡司塔

愛德，別說我這麼忍心，
拋離了你貞淑的懷抱
和恬靜的心境，
飛奔向刀叢和戰爭。

是呀，我在追求著新的愛人，
那就是殺場上第一個敵人；
我還要更熱情地擁抱
一把劍，一匹馬，一面盾。

但是這種矛盾的事情
就是你也會欽敬；
假如我不更愛榮譽不對的字
就不能給你這麼多的愛情。

一九三九年譯於重慶

To Lucasta, on Going to the Wars

Tell me not, Sweet, I am unkind,
That from the nunnery
Of thy chaste breast and quiet mind,
To war and arms I fly.

True, a new mistress now I chase,
The first foe in the field;
And with a stronger faith embrace
A sword, a horse, a shield.

Yet this inconstancy is such
As you thou too shall adore;
I could not love thee, Dear, so much,
Loved I not Honour more.

肯尼斯・費欒（Kenneth Fearing）

美國狂想曲（其四）

起初你咬你底指甲。於是你梳你底頭髮。於是你等呀又等呀。
（你知道，他們說你先是撒謊。於是他們說你偷竊。於是他們又說你殺人。）

於是門鈴響啦。於是白格來了。波邇來了。哲姻來了。達克也來了。
開始是你說話，抽煙，聽新聞，又喝了幾杯。於是你走下了樓梯。
你就吃飯，吃過後，也許就去看電影，過後就去夜總會，過後又回家來了，又爬著那樓梯，又上床睡了。

但是白格領頭爭辯起來，達克答了話。起初你跳著慣常跳的舞，喝著往常老喝的酒。
於是鋼琴在世界上建造起一個音符的屋頂
於是喇叭在空中編織成一座音樂底穹窿屋。而大鼓卻在時空和黑夜上面做成個天花板。
於是桌邊的談鋒。於是付帳。於是又回家睡了。
但是首先，那些樓梯。

於是你，乖乖的，當你爬上樓梯，你還覺得像你前回覺得回家一樣麼？

你還覺得像你今早所感覺過的麼？像昨夜麼？像前夜麼？

（你知道，他們說你首先聽到了聲音，於是你見了神兆，他們說，他們說你就踢著鬧著亂說了一泡。）

或許你覺得：在一生的許多夜裡再來一夜又算得什麼？

在兩回，三回，或四回，五回的死亡，友誼，或離婚中再來一回，又算得什麼？

在那麼多，那麼多的面孔中間再來一副面孔，在千千萬萬的生活中間再來一套生活，又算得什麼？

但是首先，乖乖的，當你爬著又數著那樓梯時（它們總是一樣多），你曾在什麼時候或什麼地方有過什麼不同的想頭麼？

乖乖的，難道這就是你生下來該這麼感覺，這麼做，和變成這麼樣麼？

一九五五年七月九日夜二時

American Rhapsody

First you bite your fingernails. And then you comb your hair
gain. And then you wait. And wait.
(They say, you know, that first you lie. And then you steal,
they say. And then, they say, you kill.)

Then the doorbell rings. Then Peg drops in. And Bill. And
Jane. And Doc.
And first you talk, and smoke, and hear the news and have a
drink. Then you walk down the stairs.
And you dine, then, and go to a show after that, perhaps, and
after that a night spot, and after that come home again,
and climb the stairs again, and again go to bed.

But first Peg argues, and Doc replies. First you dance the
same dance and you drink the same drink you always
drank before.
And the piano builds a roof of notes above the world.
And the trumpet weaves a dome of music through space. And the
drum makes a ceiling over space and time and night.
And then the table-wit. And then the check. Then home again
to bed.
But first, the stairs.

And do you now, baby, as you climb the stairs, do you still
feel as you felt back there?
Do you feel again as you felt this morning? And the night
before? And then the night before that?

(They say, you know, that first you hear voices. And then you
have visions, they say. Then, they say, you kick and
scream and rave.)

Or do you feel: What is one more night in a lifetime of nights?
What is one more death, or friendship, or divorce out of two,
or three? Or four? Or five?
One more face among so many, many faces, one more life among so
many million lives?
But first, baby, as you climb and count the stairs (and they total
the same), did you, sometime or somewhere, have a different idea?
Is this, baby, what you were born to feel, and do, and be?

阿蘭勒西
（William Edgar O'Shaughnessy）

我另外造了個花園

是啊，為了我新的「愛」
我另外造了個花園：
死了的玫瑰躺在那邊就讓牠在那邊，
我還蓋了新的在上面。
為什麼我底夏天還不來呢？
為什麼我底心兒還徘徊呢？
我「舊」的愛來了，走進這花園來了，
她把這兒蹂躪了一遍。

她帶著疲倦的笑容走進了園，
那笑容正像從前；
她把周圍望了一會
便打了個寒顫：
她經過處，對一切有如死的一觸，
她經過處，也像投了一瞥摧殘；
她使雪白的玫瑰花瓣凋落，
還把紅色的玫瑰變成了蒼白。

她慘白的衣裳拖在綠草上

如像一條長蛇

咬著那片草地！

留下了淒涼的痕跡。

她慢慢走向園門，

正像那舊時的行色，

最後她回轉身來等待，

再說了一聲訣別。

一九五三年六月四日夜深

Song

I made another garden, yea,

For my new love;

I left the dead rose where it lay,

And set the new above.

Why did the summer not begin?

Why did my heart not haste?

My old love came and walked therein,

And laid the garden waste.

She entered with her weary smile,
Just as of old;
She looked around a little while,
And shivered at the cold.
Her passing touch was death to all,
Her passing look a blight:
She made the white rose-petals fall,
And turned the red rose white.

Her pale robe, clinging to the grass,
Seemed like a snake
That bit the grass and ground, alas!
And a sad trail did make.
She went up slowly to the gate;
And there, just as of yore,
She turned back at the last to wait,
And say farewell once more.

哈代（Thomas Hardy）

他所殺死的人

要是他和我遇著
在一個古老的旅館裡，
我們早該排排並坐
喝了許多杯！

但我們已編成了軍隊，
又面對面地，狠狠地互盯著，
我就射擊他正如他也射擊我，
我把他就地殺死。

我殺死了他，因為——
因為他是我底敵人，
他當然是我底敵人，這多麼對！
這已夠簡單明白了，然而這個人

他想他入伍，也許，
只為了偶然——像我一般情景——

失了業——把行李賣去——
此外沒有原因，

是呵，戰爭是多麼古怪稀奇！
你把一個人殺死，
要是你是在酒館裡遇到他，你定會
和他攀交情，或給他幾個銅子。

一九五五年五月二十三日夜十二時

The Man He Killed

Had he and I but met
By some old ancient inn,
We should have set us down to wet
Right many a nipperkin!

But ranged as infantry,
And staring face to face,
I shot at him as he at me,
And killed him in his place.

I shot him dead because—

Because he was my foe,

Just so: my foe of course he was;

That's clear enough; although

He thought he'd 'list, perhaps,

Off-hand like—just as I—

Was out of work—had sold his traps—

No other reason why.

Yes; quaint and curious war is!

You shoot a fellow down

You'd treat, if met where any bar is,

Or help to half a crown.

散步

你近來再也不和我到
那山頂的樹邊去了，
經過通那小門的路徑
像往日的情形；
你已脆弱得不能動了，

我就獨自地去了，也沒有關心，
沒想到你是藏在後面了。

今天我又走到那樹林
懷著往日一樣的心情；
我周圍望了一望
那慣游的地方；
你這舊地重遊，
一切原來依舊，
只歸來時瞥見這寂寞的空房，
潛在的幽思完全兩樣。

一九五五年五月二十二日夜一時

The Walk

You did not walk with me
Of late to the hill-top tree
By the gated ways,
As in earlier days;
You were weak and lame,
So you never came,

And I went alone, and I did not mind,
Not thinking of you as left behind.

I walked up there to-day
Just in the former way;
Surveyed around
The familiar ground
By myself again:
What difference, then?
Only that underlying sense
Of the look of a room on returning thence.

哈得（Bret Harte）[1]

那個左道旁門的唐人
——「老實人」哲穆司的坦白話

我要用老實話
來講一講
這黑暗的賭法，
和落了空的勾當。
那個左道旁門的唐人真有點兒古怪
你是聽我來從頭講解。

他底名字叫做阿損（Ah Sin）；
我可不想否認
他這個鼎鼎的大名
也許含有別的某種意義。
但我時常對賴皮兒說道：阿損的笑真是深沉的孩子的笑。

---

[1] 【編者按】：原稿並未提供詩作原文以及作者英文原文、譯名，此處由編者所加。

那是在八月初三那一天，
天空是多麼溫和；
從這天空裡你也可以想象
阿損底個性如何。
可是他那天對老賴玩的把戲，
我卻有點而看不起。

那回我們賭了次小牌九，
阿損也來參加
我們玩的是「幽扣」（Euchre），
他本來不懂得怎麼玩法。
但他坐在桌邊滿臉笑容，
笑得那麼孩子氣和過分的謙恭。

可是老賴暗地裡砌好了牌，
這樣的勾當叫我很難過
我心裡更覺得奇怪，
他衣袖裡還藏了那麼多：
那兒塞滿了將牌和王牌，
也是為了那欺騙的買賣。

可是那個旁門左道的唐人
手裡的牌老是那麼好，
我們更是不能不吃驚
他贏得的點數又那麼高，

直到後來他出了一張最大的王牌——哪會這麼多？
這張牌老早已發給了我。

於是我把老賴直瞧，
老賴也眼巴巴對我一瞪；
他就跳起來大叫：
「這怎麼可能？
我們給廉價的華工毀啦！」——
他直撲向那左道旁門的唐人扭打。

這一場全面的武劇
我沒有參加表演，
只是滿地的紙牌飛舞，
像落葉吹散在海邊。
這是阿損在這「他不會玩的」賭博裡
所隱藏著的班底。

他那長長的衣袖套，
藏了二十四張「假克」（Jacks），
難怪他手裡的牌那麼好！
我說的全是事實；
我們還發現他尖利的指甲，
正如像「銀樣蠟搶頭」——塗滿了黏的蠟。

所以我要用老實話

來講一講

這黑暗的賭法，

和落了空的勾當，

那個左道旁門的唐人真有點兒古怪，

我一直要從頭到尾

堅持這個見解。

　　十九世紀下半期，當美國人競向西部挖金礦的時候，華僑多半以賤價勞工的身分出賣勞力。這詩描寫舊金山一帶華僑和洋人相處的生活面之一，在當時頗為流行。原文以幽默見勝。

一九五三年五月二十七日

The Heathen Chinee

Which I wish to remark—

And my language is plain—

That for ways that are dark

And for tricks that are vain,

The heathen Chinee is peculiar

Which the same I would rise to explain.

Ah Sin was his name;

And I shall not deny

In regard to the same

What his name might implyl

But his smile it was pensive and childlike,

As I frequent remarked to Bill Nye.

It was August the third;

And quite soft was the skies;

Which it might be inferred

That Ah Sin was likewise;

Yet he played it that day upon William

And me in a way I despise.

Which we had a small game,

And Ah Sin took a hand;

It was Euchre, the game,

He did not understand;

But he smiled as he sat by the table,

With the smile that was childlike and bland.

Yet the cards they were stacked

In a way that I grieve,

And my feelings were shocked

At the state of Nye's sleeve;

Which was stuffed full of aces and bowers,

And the same with intent to deceive.

But the hands that were played

By that heathen Chinee,

And the points that he made,

Were quite frightful to see—

Till at last he put down a right bowers,

Which the same Nye had dealt unto me.

Then I looked up at Nye,

And he gazed upon me;

And he rose with a sigh,

And said, "Can this be? We are ruined by Chinese cheap labor"—

And he went to that heathen Chinee.

In the scene that ensued

I did not take a hand

But the floor it was strewed

Like the leaves on the strand

With the cards that Ah Sin had been hiding,

In the game "he did not understand."

In his sleeves, which were long,

He had twenty-four packs—

Which was coming it strong,

Yet I state but the facts;

And we found on his nails, which were toper,

What is frequent in paper— that's wax.

Which is why I remark,

And my language is plain,

That for ways that are dark,

And for tricks that are vain,

The heathen Chinee is peculiar—

Which the same I am free to maintain

哈爾特・克倫（Hart Crane）

夢爾維爾墓畔作

他看到，常在暗礁邊，波濤下，
溺死者骸骨做的骰子遺留給縱橫家。
他看到那上面的數字
拋擲在塵岸上，模糊了。

而船骸飄過沒有鈴聲，
死之恩賜底花萼送回來
散了的一章，寫著鉛色的象形文字
那凶兆在貝殼的走廊裡受了傷。

於是在大漩渦平靜的周圍
它底譴責降服了，要惡意妥協了，
有冰霜的眼抬高了祭壇；
有沉默的回答爬過了星空。

羅盤和航海儀不再創設
風潮……那高峻的蒼翠的懸崖上
挽歌不可喚醒這海客
他傳奇的英靈只埋在海裡

一九五六年十二月二十二日夜十二時

At Melvilie's Tomb

Often beneath the wave, wide from this ledge
The dice of drowned men's bones he saw bequeath
An embassy. Their numbers as he watched,
Beat on the dusty shore and were obscured.

And wrecks passed without sound of bells,
The calyx of death's bounty giving back
A scattered chapter, livid hieroglyph,
The portent wound in corridors of shells.

Then in the circuit calm of one vast coil,
Its lashings charmed and malice reconciled,

Frosted eyes there were that lifted altars;
And silent answers crept across the stars.

Compass, quadrant and sextant contrive
No farther tides... High in the azure steeps
Monody shall not wake the mariner.
This fabulous shadow only the sea keeps.

威廉・阿林漢（Allingham）

憶

兩對鴨兒在池塘，
隔岸是綠草芬芳，
春天蔚藍的天上
白雲展翅飛翔；
這小小的好風光
叫人永遠不能忘──
想起就眼淚汪汪！

一九五六年十二月十日下午六時譯於 Sumner Road, Cambridge, Mass

A Memory

Four ducks on a pond,

A grass-bank beyond,

A blue sky of spring,

White clouds on the wing;

What a little thing

To remember for years—

To remember with tears!

拜倫（Lord George Gordon Byron）

大海

無路的森林裡有的是歡喜，
孤另的海岸上有的是狂歡，
絕無人跡出境卻有集會
海邊濤聲裡是音樂在震顫。
我不是少愛人類，而是更愛自然，
在這些境界裡我們相遇見，
我就暗地裡把未來或過去的我拋遠，
和大宇宙交溶在一處，
感到多麼表現不出的，卻無法掩飾的情趣。

滾向前去，你深沉的碧海啊，滾！
萬個艦隊也掃蕩不了你一片汪洋；
人類用廢墟把陸地畫了傷痕，──
他底統治只限於岸上；──
水面的碎片才是你業績底輝煌，
人類除了遺骸沒遺留一絲蹤影，

只有那一剎那間，像一滴雨一樣，
沸騰地呻吟著沉沒到你底波心，
沒有個墳墓，不敲聲喪鐘，未曾棺殮，也永遠無名。

人底腳步沒踏過到你底路上——
你底地盤不是他所能劫剝掠的東西，——
你起來把他趕離了身旁；
他用來摧毀陸地的威力在你眼裡拋在空中浮長，
在你戲弄的浪花中戰慄悲傷，
你送他去和他底星星，作伴，
那附近的港口也許有他小小的希望，
你把他摔到地上：——在那而埋葬。

大砲像雷霆般霹擊石頭的城牆，
叫萬國都在牠面前發抖，
也震懾了都城裡的國王；
橡木戰艦底胸口挺著巨大的骨頭，
使創造泥土的人類虛聲誇口，
誇說是你底主宰和戰爭底仲裁，——
這些都不過是你底玩具，
像雪片在你浪花底泡沫裡溶解，
你把無敵艦隊底驕傲和英國底戰利品一齊毀壞。

你岸上的帝國哪能和你一樣不變；
亞述，希臘，羅馬，迦太基，哪兒還有蹤影？

牠們自由時你底潮水沖給他們威權；
也沖給他們無數的暴君；
他們底國土屈服於外族，奴隸，或野蠻的人們；
他們底衰亡把錦繡江山變成了沙漠的枯境，
除了狂濤底戲弄，只你是不變而永恆，
時間在你蔚藍的額上寫不了皺紋，
你總像創造底黎明，向前直滾。

你啊，你是面輝煌的寶鏡，
在風暴裡把全能的造物者照出了原形；
無論是和風的恬靜或暴風雨的震驚，
是寒凝把北極或是在赤熱裡神祕翻騰；
你該是一片汪洋，莊嚴壯麗而無盡，
你啊，你是永恆底象徵，
好一座幽冥無形王位。
你底黏淀造成了水底的巨靈；
你統治一切；可怕地，無底地，孤獨地前進。

啊，大海！我向來就愛你，
我小時多麼喜歡躺在你懷裡！
像你底泡沫般向前澎湃；擁擠；
和那般破浪的船舶遊戲，——
那船舶真讓我滿心歡喜，雖有些恐怖
破浪震蕩時
因為我就是你底孩子

無論到海角天涯都信賴你底波濤，
永遠像現在一樣，用手來撫摸你底鬃毛

一九五七年四月十三日

The Sea[1]

There is a pleasure in the pathless woods,
　　There is a rapture on the lonely shore,
　　There is society where none intrudes
　　By the deep sea, and music in its roar:
　　I love not man the less, but nature more,
　　From these our interviews, in which I steal
　　From all I may be, or have been before,
　　To mingle with the universe, and feel
What I can ne'er express, yet cannot all conceal.

　　Roll on, thou deep and dark blue Ocean,—roll!
　　Ten thousand fleets sweep over thee in vain;
　　Man marks the earth with ruin,—his control

---

[1] 【編者按】：此詩英文原文為編者所加，原書稿缺。

Stops with the shore;—upon the watery plain
The wrecks are all thy deed, nor doth remain
A shadow of man's ravage, save his own,
When, for a moment, like a drop of rain,
He sinks into thy depths with bubbling groan,
Without a grave, unknelled, uncoffined, and unknown.

His steps are not upon thy paths,—thy fields
Are not a spoil for him,—thou dost arise
And shake him from thee; the vile strength he wields
For earth's destruction thou dost all despise,
Spurning him from thy bosom to the skies,
And send'st him, shivering in thy playful spray
And howling, to his gods, where haply lies
His petty hope in some near port or bay,
And dashest him again to earth:—there let him lay.

The armaments which thunderstrike the walls
Of rock-built cities, bidding nations quake
And monarchs tremble in their capitals,
The oak leviathans, whose huge ribs make
Their clay creator the vain title take
Of lord of thee and arbiter of war,—
These are thy toys, and, as the snowy flake,
They melt into thy yeast of waves, which mar
Alike the Armada's pride or spoils of Trafalgar.

Thy shores are empires, changed in all save thee;

Assyria, Greece, Rome, Carthage, what are they?

Thy waters wasted them while they were free,

And many a tyrant since; their shores obey

The stranger, slave, or savage; their decay

Has dried up realms to deserts: not so thou;

Unchangeable save to thy wild waves' play,

Time writes no wrinkles on thine azure brow;

Such as creation's dawn beheld, thou rollest now.

Thou glorious mirror, where the Almighty's form

Glasses itself in tempests; in all time,

Calm or convulsed,—in breeze, or gale, or storm,

Icing the pole, or in the torrid clime

Dark-heaving; boundless, endless, and sublime,

The image of Eternity,—the throne

Of the Invisible! even from out thy slime

The monsters of the deep are made; each zone

Obeys thee; thou goest forth, dread, fathomless, alone.

And I have loved thee, Ocean! and my joy

Of youthful sports was on thy breast to be

Borne, like thy bubbles, onward; from a boy

I wantoned with thy breakers,—they to me

Were a delight; and if the freshening sea

Made them a terror, 't was a pleasing fear;

For I was as it were a child of thee,

And trusted to thy billows far and near,

And laid my hand upon thy mane,—as I do here.

弔羅馬

羅馬呵！我的故國！你這靈魂之城！

赤心的孤兒們都要歸依你，

你是死去的帝國孤另的母親！

孤兒們要在鬱塞的心胸裡把微細的悲痛抑制，

我們的災殃和苦難比起你來還有什麼要緊，

來吧，來聽這貓頭鷹，來看這古柏，

來用沉重的腳生踏在這破敗的神廟和王座的階庭，

你們呵，你們的劇痛只算得一日的折磨——

在我們腳下卻有個世界像黏土般脆弱。

這以帝國為殤女的堯卜呵！她站在這兒老態龍鍾，

喪失了孩子，喪失了鳳冠，只浸沉在無聲的悲哀裡；

枯萎的雙手捧著一隻空空的屍夾甕，

裡面的骨灰在許久以前就已散失；

色驃族的荒墳於今已不再埋有遺骸；

這墳墓在那兒寂寞地躺著，
牠往日住過的的英雄們而今安在？
太白河呵！你還流過這大理石的荒野麼？
起來，用你黃色的波濤，掩埋她的痛苦折磨。

高斯人，基督徒，時代，戰爭，洪水，和火災，
摧殘了這七丘之城的驕傲；
她親眼看到光榮像一顆星一顆星般沉埋；
那兒是蠻夷降王慣經過的馳道，
素車白馬從那裡馳驅到朱比特神殿，
如今這遙遠壯闊的廟宇都已崩頹得不留痕跡，
只一片混亂的廢墟！還有誰來發掘這荒原，
有誰來向這敗瓦頹垣上投一線慘澹的眼色，
有誰來說：「這兒曾經，或者正是」？這兒呀，只有雙重的黑夜！

這時代和她的雙重黑夜，這夜之女兒昧愚，
曾經蒙蔽，而且現在還蒙蔽著我們：
我們只摸索著自己的路走向錯誤：
原來大海也有圖，繁星也有文，
智識把牠們分布在她寬闊的裙裾上；
但是羅馬卻像一片沙漠的荒境在這裡
我們只踏著弔古的憂傷
卻拍手叫道：「我發現了！」可是明明
只是廢墟的海市蜃樓現了形影。

呀！呀！這高尚的古都！

那歷史上三百次大勝利早已成了空虛，

那日子哪兒去了？當布魯達斯底七首一擊便奪去

征服者寶劍所得的榮譽！

呀！西賽羅底雄辯，浮吉爾底詩歌，

和李維繪聲繪影的史頁！——這些都將

使羅馬復活；除了這，就只有——衰落。

呀！在現世裡我們已不能夢想

再見到羅馬自由時她眼睛裡的晶亮！

一九五五年七月十六日下午五時

另譯：

弔羅馬

1

嗟羅馬吾故國兮，

實靈府之首都。

古帝國紛紛其夭殤兮，

唯餘此孤母。

孽子孤臣無所依兮，

宜傾心而向汝。

念汝之奇愁已潰蕩兮，

我抑塞之微憂其可忘。

覽古柏兮蒼蒼，

聽夜梟兮啼聲長。
登故宮之荒階兮，
步趑趄而難安，
吾終身之憂兮，
其促也如一日之患。
對此一片茫茫兮，
感萬物之脆弱易殘。

2

彼絕國兮，不復存兮，
喪明之孤母，復何榮兮！
既獨立兮熒熒，
亦痛哭兮失聲。
慨屍灰能久已零落兮，
撫空棺而一慟；
色驃族之荒墳何纍纍兮，
覓遺骸而無蹤。
彼一世之雄兮
而今安在？
豈太白之河兮
長流於此白石之荒外？
汝洪濤其滾滾兮，
其淹汲此終古之遺憾兮！

3

既見摧兮於高斯之族，
又蹂躪於基督景教之徒，
日月推儀已代謝兮，
況刀兵水火之荼毒，
宜乎此七丘之城兮，
已慘澹而不驕，
睹聲華之消沉兮，
如大星之西凋。
昔者兮諸蠻夷之王，
乘素車兮堂堂，
此蕩蕩之馳道兮，
趨神殿以即受降。
奈何此樓閣兮崩裂無餘，
亂紛紛兮唯有廢墟！
誰復顧此敗瓦頹垣兮，
誇舊烈而悼今衰？
惟荒原之漠漠兮，
夜陰陰而沉霾。

4

蕭條異代兮夜已深，
汝之身世兮夜愈陰沉。
此垂夜之愚暗兮黑幕層久，
使舉世兮不復醒。

我徘徊於歧路兮，
終迷失於乖誤兮。
吾固知繁星兮有文，大海兮有圖，
彼智慧之仙娥固盈盈兮，
亦嘗示我以坦途；
惜羅馬已荒敗兮，
我徒顛沛於此遺墟，
拾碎屑瓦殘磚而歡呼兮，
猶獲謂有所悟也，──
不知其為海市蜃樓兮，
實虛妄而無挺也。

5
吁嗟乎！汝華嚴之古都兮，
盛世之兵威，只今何處兮？
昔布魯達斯之匕首一擊兮，
曾使暴君之利劍無所施其技兮！
吁嗟乎！
西賽羅之雄辯滔滔，
浮吉爾之詩華矯矯，
益以李維繪聲繪影之史頁，
誠令古羅馬兮栩栩欲活。
此諸烈既業已不存兮，
信此邦之衰竭。
吁嗟乎！羅馬不復自由，

往日之明眸空燦燦爛兮，
雖寢寐亦不可求！

一九五六年十月九日夜二時，一小時內譯成。

Rome

Oh Rome! my country! city of the soul!
   The orphans of the heart must turn to thee,
   Lone mother of dead empires! and control
   In their shut breasts their petty misery.
   What are our woes and sufferance? Come and see
   The cypress, hear the owl, and plod your way
   O'er steps of broken thrones and temples, Ye!
   Whose agonies are evils of day—
A world is at our feet as fragile as our clay.

   The Niobe of nations! there she stands,
   Childless and crownless, in her voiceless woe;
   An empty urn within her wither'd hands,
   Whose holy dust was scatter'd long ago;
   The Scipios' tomb contains no ashes now;

The very sepulchres lie tenantless

Of their heroic dwellers: dost thou flow,

Old Tiber! through a marble wilderness?

Rise, with thy yellow waves, and mantle her distress.

The Goth, the Christian, Time, War, Flood and Fire

Have dealt upon the seven-hill'd city's pride;

She saw her glories star by star expire,

And up the steep barbarian monarchs ride,

Where the car climb'd the capitol; far and wide

Temple and Tower went down, nor left a site:—

Chaos of ruins! Who shall trace the void,

O'er the dim fragments cast a lunar light,

And say, "here was, or is," where all is doubly night?

The double night of ages, and of her,

Night's daughter, Ignorance, hath wrapt, and wrap

All round us; we but feel our way to err:

The ocean hath its chart, the stars their map;

And knowledge spreads them on her ample lap;

But Rome is as the desert, where we steer

Stumbling o'er recollections: now we clap

Our hands, and cry, 'Eureka!' it is clear—

When but some false mirage of ruin rises near.

Alas, the lofty city! and alas

The trebly hundred triumphs! and the day

When Brutus made the dagger's edge surpass

The conqueror's sword in bearing fame away!

Alas for Tully's voice, and Virgil's lay,

And Livy's pictured page! But these shall be

Her resurrection; all beside—decay.

Alas for Earth, for never shall we see

That brightness in her eye she bore when Rome was free!

—From *Childe Harold's Pilgrimage*, Canto the fourth, LXXVIII-LXXXII. Written at Venice between June of 1817 and January of 1818 and published immediately.

她蹣跚漫步

她蹣跚漫步，

像一夜，星空下萬里無雲，

一切最美好的暗淡光明

都在她臉上和眼波裡相遇，

就這樣成熟了溫柔的光彩，

天空卻不肯把它賜給濃豔的白天。

增一絲影子就太多，減一絲光線就太少，
都會損傷她一半無名的美妙。
這美妙波動在她烏黑的雲鬢上，
有時候輕輕映在她底臉龐，
那兒沉思表現著寧靜的甜蜜，
一個多麼純潔，多麼可愛的地方，

在這豐頰和秀眉上
那麼溫柔，恬靜，又會說話，
贏人的微笑，爛漫的色調，
正說出了歡喜中度過的時光，
說出了一種平靜的心情，
和一顆心有著天真的愛情。

一九五五年六月二十四日下午三時

　　這兒的她指拜倫底表妹Lady Wilmot Harton。他在一八一四年
六月一個舞會上遇見她，這時她還居喪，衣上飾著銀色的花片。

She Walks In Beauty

She walks in beauty, like the night
Of cloudless climes and starry skies;
And all that's best of dark and bright
Meet in her aspect and her eyes:
Thus mellowed to that tender light
Which heaven to gaudy day denies.

One shade the more, one ray the less,
Had half impaired the nameless grace
Which waves in every raven tress
Or softly lightens o'er her face;
Where thoughts serenely sweet express
How pure, how dear their dwelling-place.

And on that cheek, and o'er that brow
So soft, so calm, yet eloquent,
The smiles that win, the tints that glow,
But tell of days in goodness spent,
A mind at peace with all below,
A heart whose love is innocent.

別湯穆斯・莫爾

（一）
我底小艇在岸邊，
我底航船在海上；
但是湯穆啊，在我離別之前，
這兒要祝你健康！

（二）
愛我的，我給他們一歎，
恨我的，我給他們一笑；
不管前途怎麼艱難，
我有一顆心兒去應付任何逆道。

（三）
雖然大海圍著我狂嘯，
但它說會把我載走；
雖然將有一片沙漠在我周遭，
那兒總會有泉水飄流。

（四）
即使那井裡只有最後一滴甘泉，
當我喘息在那井邊，精力都已枯盡，

在我底心靈昏絕之前，
我寧願為你而祝飲。

（五）
這杯酒，就像那枯泉，
要是我能禱祝你我底平安，
湯穆啊，還有你底強健，
我願把它一飲而乾。

一九五一年九月十四日

另譯：

別夜

（一）
小舟艤岸，
征航在海；
賤子將行，
酌我金罍！

（二）
愛我者，報之一歎，
恨我者，報之笑顏；
前路茫茫，
我心孔安。

（三）
滄海狂嘯，
克載前驅；
絕漠雖遙，
清泉可掬。

（四）
枯泉一滴，
我渴且死，
為君一別，
式甘飲此。

（五）
我飲此酒，
如彼枯泉；
願共平安，
且祝君健。

一九四〇年譯於重慶

To Thomas Moor

1

My boat is on the shore,

And my bark is on the sea;

But, before I go, Tom Moore,

Here's a double health to thee!

2

Here's a sigh to those who love me,

And a smile to those who hate;

And, whatever sky's above me,

Here's a heart for every fate.

3

Though the ocean roar around me,

Yet it still shall bear me on;

Though a desert should surround me,

It hath springs that may be won.

4

Were't the last drop in the well,

As I gasp'd upon the brink,

Ere my fainting spirit fell,

'Tis to thee that I would drink.

風媒集：
周策縱翻譯詩集

180

5

With that water, as this wine,

The libation I would pour

Should be—peace with thine and mine,

And a health to thee, Tom Moore!

哀希臘

1

希臘群島呵，希臘群島！

熱戀的沙浮在你這兒唱過情歌，

你孕育過輝煌的武術和文教，

湧出過德羅斯島，生長過亞坡羅！

於今這永恆的夏天還替你鍍著金光，

可是那往日的一切都已沒落，只餘下了太陽。

2

凱俄斯和特奧斯的兩位詩人，

用英雄底豎琴和情人底琵琶，

在海外贏得了不朽的名聲；

只有這沉寂的故鄉反把它抹煞，

你不管這名聲早已在西方響遍，

比你祖先底「極樂島」還遙遠。

3

群山面對著馬拉松古戰場——
馬拉松古戰場面對著海洋；
我獨自在這兒徘徊默想，
夢想著希臘也許還是個自由的城邦；
我腳踏著波斯人底墳地，
終不能設想自己是個奴隸。

4

在那俯瞰沙拉米斯的懸崖上
曾經高坐著一個波斯國王；
那下面有成千的兵艦排列成行，
還有無數的大軍；——都歸他手掌
天剛剛亮時他還把他們點數——
太陽落下時，他們就蹤影全無！

5

他們底蹤影在什麼地方？
我底祖國呵，你又在什麼地方？
在你沉默的國土上，英雄的歌曲早已銷亡——
英雄的胸膛早已不再跳盪！
難道你自古以來高潔的詩琴
定要淪落到我手中來彈出哀音？

6

我寧願和戴了枷鎖的民族在一起，
雖然這不是甚麼光榮，
我只要能感到愛國者底羞恥，
連歌唱時也會羞得臉上紅暈；
到底是為了什麼，詩人還留在這裡？
給希臘人一點羞，給希臘一滴眼淚。

7

難道我們只該痛哭往日的成敗？
難道我們只該愧對祖宗流過的鮮血？
大地呵！請你把懷抱打開，
交還我一些斯巴達底遺烈！
三百壯士裡只要你交還三位，
來再造一次瘦馬披離關口的光輝！

8

怎麼呀，還只有沉默？全是沉默？
哦！不；——這兒有的是死者底聲音
響得像遙遠的瀑布，
答應說：「只要還有一個活人，
只要一個起來，我們就來響應，響應！」
可是呵只這活人卻啞口無聲。

9

枉然，枉然：且讓我把絃音調換；
把高杯斟滿沙摩斯美酒！
對土耳其侵異者且不用管，
讓凱俄斯底葡萄血酒儘流！
聽吧！對那淫歌蕩舞的召喚，
每個放浪的酒鬼是多麼狂歡！

10

你們只有鬪雷克舞蹈，
哪裡還有鬪雷克戰陣？
在這兩種本事中為什麼只忘掉
那高貴而威武的一門？
你們有卡謨斯介紹來的文字——
難道他是要教給一個奴隸？

11

把大碗斟滿沙摩斯美酒！
莫讓這弔古的幽情來叫我們擔憂！
美酒曾使安納克倫底詩歌神妙不朽；
他卻只侍候在暴君卜利克提斯左右；
那時我們底主人雖然專暴，
卻至少還是本國的同胞。

12

寇森尼斯底那個暴君
對自由反稱是最勇敢的好友；
米爾塔提斯是他底大名！
唉！今天我們寧願再有
再有同樣勇武的暴君
他那種鐵鏈必然能把我們縈緊。

13

把大碗斟滿沙摩斯美酒！
在蘇里山崖上，在帕加海岸上，
有一支英雄的種族遺留，
它和陶內安後裔相像；
那兒也許撒播著自由的種子，
使赫寇力士的血統永遠得嗣。

14

切莫把自由信託給西歐的人們，
他們底國王只講買賣；
只有祖國的刀槍和祖國的兵，
纔寄託著英勇底期待：
但當心土耳其和拉丁的狡猾，
要來改攻破你堅固的盾牌。

15

把大碗斟滿沙摩斯美酒！

美麗的姑娘樹蔭下依然有歡舞

我對著這一個個容光煥發的少女，

看見她們閃爍漆黑的眼珠

怎禁得住自己滿眶的熱淚，

一想到這樣的乳房都要去餵奴隸。

16

請讓我攀登蘇尼謨大理石的懸崖，

那兒只我與波濤作伴，

你可聽到我和濤聲對白；

我將放歌而死像天邊的鴻雁：

奴隸國決不是我底家鄉——

摔掉這杯沙摩斯美酒不嘗！

一九五六年十月二日五時，譯完於20 Sumner Rd., Cambridge, Mass

The Isles of Greece[2]

The isles of Greece! the isles of Greece
    Where burning Sappho loved and sung,
Where grew the arts of war and peace,
    Where Delos rose, and Phoebus sprung!
Eternal summer gilds them yet,
But all, except their sun, is set.

The Scian and the Teian muse,
    The hero's harp, the lover's lute,
Have found the fame your shores refuse:
    Their place of birth alone is mute
To sounds which echo further west
Than your sires' 'Islands of the Blest.

The mountains look on Marathon—
    And Marathon looks on the sea;
And musing there an hour alone,
    I dream'd that Greece might still be free;
For standing on the Persians' grave,
I could not deem myself a slave.

---

[2] 【編者按】：此詩英文原文為編者所加，原書稿缺。

A king sate on the rocky brow
　　Which looks o'er sea-born Salamis;
And ships, by thousands, lay below,
　　And men in nations;—all were his!
He counted them at break of day—
And when the sun set, where were they?

And where are they? and where art thou,
　　My country? On thy voiceless shore
The heroic lay is tuneless now—
　　The heroic bosom beats no more!
And must thy lyre, so long divine,
Degenerate into hands like mine?

'Tis something in the dearth of fame,
　　Though link'd among a fetter'd race,
To feel at least a patriot's shame,
　　Even as I sing, suffuse my face;
For what is left the poet here?
For Greeks a blush—for Greece a tear.

Must we but weep o'er days more blest?
　　Must we but blush?—Our fathers bled.
Earth! render back from out thy breast
　　A remnant of our Spartan dead!

Of the three hundred grant but three,

To make a new Thermopylae!

What, silent still? and silent all?

 Ah! no;—the voices of the dead

Sound like a distant torrent's fall,

 And answer, 'Let one living head,

But one, arise,—we come, we come!'

'Tis but the living who are dumb.

In vain—in vain: strike other chords;

 Fill high the cup with Samian wine!

Leave battles to the Turkish hordes,

 And shed the blood of Scio's vine:

Hark! rising to the ignoble call—

How answers each bold Bacchanal!

You have the Pyrrhic dance as yet;

 Where is the Pyrrhic phalanx gone?

Of two such lessons, why forget

 The nobler and the manlier one?

You have the letters Cadmus gave—

Think ye he meant them for a slave?

Fill high the bowl with Samian wine!

 We will not think of themes like these!

It made Anacreon's song divine:

    He served—but served Polycrates—

A tyrant; but our masters then

Were still, at least, our countrymen.

The tyrant of the Chersonese

    Was freedom's best and bravest friend;

That tyrant was Miltiades!

    O that the present hour would lend

Another despot of the kind!

Such chains as his were sure to bind.

Fill high the bowl with Samian wine!

    On Suli's rock, and Parga's shore,

Exists the remnant of a line

    Such as the Doric mothers bore;

And there, perhaps, some seed is sown,

The Heracleidan blood might own.

Trust not for freedom to the Franks—

    They have a king who buys and sells;

In native swords and native ranks

    The only hope of courage dwells:

But Turkish force and Latin fraud

Would break your shield, however broad.

Fill high the bowl with Samian wine!
　　Our virgins dance beneath the shade—
I see their glorious black eyes shine;
　　But gazing on each glowing maid,
My own the burning tear-drop laves,
To think such breasts must suckle slaves.

Place me on Sunium's marbled steep,
　　Where nothing, save the waves and I,
May hear our mutual murmurs sweep;
　　There, swan-like, let me sing and die:
A land of slaves shall ne'er be mine—
Dash down yon cup of Samian wine!

留別雅典女郎

Ζωή μου, σᾶς ἀγαπῶ.
「我底生命，我戀愛你。」

雅典女郎呵，在我們別離的時辰，
還我呀，還我底心！
或者，因我底心早已離了胸臆，

你就保留它吧，還索性要了我其餘的一切！
請聽我臨去時發個誓：
「我底生命，我戀愛你。」

對你那蓬鬆的鬢髮，
愛琴海的風吹著吹婚的情話；
你那像墨玉色流蘇的睫毛
吻著你柔軟的雙頰上開花的臉潮；
你還有魚卵般透明的眼珠──呀，讓這些都來證實：
「我底生命，我戀愛你。」

你那朱脣呀我渴望一嘗；
羅帶輕輕圍在你纖腰上；
那定情的花朵訴說了
連語言也不能說得那麼好的情調；
還有，愛情產生了悲歡──呀，讓這些都來證實：
「我底生命，我戀愛你。」

雅典女郎呵，我就要去了呵，
當你孤獨時，愛的喲，千萬想起我！
雖然我已飛去了伊斯坦堡城，
雅典卻留住我整個的心靈：
我能中斷對你的愛情麼？我只答個不字！
「我底生命，我戀愛你。」

一九五五年七月十七日下午六時

"Maid of Athens, Ere We Part"

Maid of Athens, ere we part,
Give, oh, give back my heart!
Or, since that has left my breast,
Keep it now, and take the rest!
Hear my vow before I go,
Ζωή μου, σᾶς ἀγαπῶ.

By those tresses unconfined,
Wooed by each Aegean wind;
By those lids whose jetty fringe
Kiss thy soft cheeks' blooming tinge;
By those wild eyes like the roe,
Ζωή μου, σᾶς ἀγαπῶ.

By that lip I long to taste;
By that zone-encircled waist;
By all the token-flowers that tell
What words can never speak so well;
By love's alternate joy and woe,
Ζωή μου, σᾶς ἀγαπῶ.

Maid of Athens! I am gone:
Think of me, sweet! When alone.

Though I fly to Istambol,
Athens holds my heart and soul:
Can I cease to love thee? No!
Ζωή μου, σᾶς ἀγαπῶ.

附蘇曼殊譯〈留別雅典女郎〉

夭夭雅典女，去去傷離別。
還儂肺與肝，為君久摧折！
薰修始自今，更締同心結。
臨行進一辭，吾生誓相悅！

鬈髮未及笄，九曲如腸結。
垂睫水晶簾，秋波映澄澈。
駢首試香頮，花染臙脂雪。
慧眼雙明珠，吾生誓相悅！

朱脣生異香，猥近儂情切。
錦帶束纖腰，中作鴛鴦結。
擷花遺所思，微妙超言說。
痴愛起悲歡，吾生誓相悅！

夭夭雅典女，儂去影形滅。
會當寂寥時，相念毋中絕！
儂身不可留，馳驅向突厥。
魂魄持贈君，永與柔腸結。
此情無窮期，吾生誓相悅！

（見《拜倫詩選》，發刊於民元前六年，出版於東京三秀舍。）

柯立芝（Hartley Coleridge）

短歌

她的外表平凡，
像許多女郎一般，
直到她對我一笑，
我從未發覺她的可愛；
於是我看出她的眼睛多麼明亮，
是一井的愛，一泉的光！

現在她變羞澀而冷淡，
眼皮再也不向我回轉，
可是我卻一直看透
她眼裡有愛的光輝
每當她眉頭一皺
卻比別的女郎滿面笑容還嫵媚。

一九五五年七月四日

Song

She is not fair to outward view,
As many maidens be,
Her loveliness I never knew
Until she smiled on me;
O, then I saw her eye was bright,
A well of love, a spring of light.

But now her looks are coy and cold;
To mine they ne'er reply,
And yet I cease not to behold,
The love-light in her eye:
Her very frowns are better far
Than smiles of other maidens are.

約翰・馬斯菲爾德（John Masefield）

我想到天空就失了眠

我想到天空就失了眠，
那無限的天空，充滿著億萬個星球，
行星永遠在虛無中旋轉，
彗星戴著火樣的頭髮奔走。
要使我能航行到那虛無中，
我將伴著暗淡的繁星，穿過靜默和真空，
於是在黑暗裡看見一點光彩
燒得紅光閃爍，凝做一塊，
和流浪的行星溶成一個太陽。
我超過了牠再向前進，
就看見牠餘光照在落月底花岡石上，
然後死在黑暗裡，這纔是真正的夜來臨。
這一夜，我心靈許是在虛無裡
航行了百萬年，那兒甚至沒有死，也沒有眼淚。

一九五五年六月二十六日下午二時半

I Could Not Sleep For Thinking Of The Sky

I could not sleep for thinking of the sky,
The unending sky, with all its million suns
Which turn their planets everlastingly
In nothing, where the fire-haired comet runs.
If I could sail that nothing, I should cross
Silence and emptiness with dark stars passing,
Then, in the darkness, see a point of gloss
Burn to a glow, and glare, and keep amassing,
And rage into a sun with wandering planets
And drop behind, and then, as I proceed,
See his last light upon his last moon's granites
Die to dark that would be night indeed.
Night where my soul might sail a million years
In nothing, not even death, not even tears.

和她做了朋友

和她做了朋友，我就不在乎，
不在乎神們或人們來虐待我，打擊我；
她底話就像星星，夠我去旅行，
我把她沉默的讚美當作皇冠樣的光榮。

和她做了朋友，我並不貪望黃金，
只望有件莊嚴的禮物來討她底歡心；
和她坐在一起，牽住她底手，
這就是財富，勝過了滿箱得金銀。

和她做了朋友，我只貪望美術，
潔白的情焰會來和我聯在一起，
我用跳動的心，探索那寫在她臉上
彎彎曲曲的文字，那歌頌美麗的讚美詩。

一九五三年十二月二日夜一時

Being Her Friend

Being her friend, I do not care, not I,

How gods or men may wrong me, beat me down;

Her word's sufficient star to travel by,

I count her quiet praise sufficient crown.

Being her friend, I do not covet gold,

Save a royal gift to give her pleasure;

To sit with her, and have her hand to hold,

Is wealth, I think, surpassing minted treasure.

Being her friend, I only covet art,

A white pure flame to search me as I trace

In crooked letters from a throbbing heart

The hymn to beauty written on her face.

奉神曲

不是為了王公和教主，他們有戴著假髮的車夫
駕駛著他們得意洋洋地走向榮譽，舐盡了年年的豐收，──
而是為了那被侮辱了的──被拋棄了的一團困在刀槍裡的小人物。

為了那戰鬥到死的潰散了的士兵，
他們在戰塵裡，吶喊裡，和炮聲裡昏沉。
為了那頭顱破碎，眼睛充滿了血絲的人們。

不是為了掛滿勛章的指揮官，他們被帝王寵信，
在號角聲中騎著高頭大馬遊行，
而是為了那背著槍的無名的壯丁。

我不為統治者，而是為了小兵，路上的流浪人，
為了捐著布袋，被刺棒驅趕著的奴隸們，
為了有太重的負擔，過於困倦了的人。

為了水手，汽船上添煤炭的工人，和衣衫襤褸者，
為了桅索旁俯身的歌唱者，
為了輪機邊昏昏欲睡的工人，和疲倦的瞭望著。

別人也許歌頌美酒，財富，和愉快，
歌頌著冠傳帶的元首威風凜凜的儀態；——
我卻歌頌著骯髒和渣滓，泥土和塵埃。

他們底是音樂，色彩，榮耀，和黃金；
我底是一抓糞土和微塵。
為了淒冷雨裡殘廢的，跛了的，瞎了的人們——
我底歌為他們而唱，我底故事為他們而說。阿門。

一九五五年六月二十五日夜一時

A Consecration

Not of the princes and prelates with periwigged charioteers
Riding triumphantly laurelled to lap the fat of the years,—
Rather the scorned—the rejected—the men hemmed in with the spears;

The men of the tattered battalion which fights till it dies,
Dazed with the dust of the battle, the din and the cries.
The men with the broken heads and the blood running into their eyes.

Not the be-medalled Commander, beloved of the throne,
Riding cock-horse to parade when the bugles are blown,
But the lads who carried the koppie and cannot be known.
Not the ruler for me, but the ranker, the tramp of the road,
The slave with the sack on his shoulders pricked on with the goad,
The man with too weighty a burden, too weary a load.

The sailor, the stoker of steamers, the man with the clout,
The chantyman bent at the halliards putting a tune to the shout,
The drowsy man at the wheel and the tired look-out.

Others may sing of the wine and the wealth and the mirth,
The portly presence of potentates goodly in girth;—
Mine be the dirt and the dross, the dust and scum of the earth!

Theirs be the music, the colour, the glory, the gold;

Mine be a handful of ashes, a mouthful of mould.

Of the maimed, of the halt and the blind in the rain and the cold—

Of these shall my songs be fashioned, my tales be told.

Amen.

澤國之夜

夜來到了澤國之裡，來到了孤另的荒原上，

來到了小山中，那兒風吹著牛羊吃過的青草，

青草倒壓在未曾犁過的瘠地上，

松濤怒吼像拍岸的浪潮。

這裡羅馬人曾孤寂地生活在淒風荒蕪裡，

於今是暗淡了，只有野雉出沒無常；

再也沒有生物的蹤跡，除了黑頭的鷗鳥，

和貓頭鷹底如撲火燈蛾般的死亡。

在這甲蟲低吟的澤國裡有的是「美」；

從羅馬城區中太白河邊的宮殿

到這涼風吹掃的無名荒山，

叫人想起身披紫袍的凱撒。

這兒荒涼的「美」伴著憂鬱，
像心靈前線上英勇的思緒，
像在瘋狂的行軍中曠野的營房裡
「盲目皇后」明亮的眼珠。

於今有過「美」的地方就有風凋了的金雀花，
牠像老人在山風呼嘯中呻吟；
飛揚的天空灰暗裡有奔馬，
夜充滿了往古的友情。

一九五五年六月二十五日夜十二時

Night On The Downland

Night is on the downland, on the lonely moorland,
On the hills where the wind goes over sheep-bitten turf,
Where the bent grass beats upon the unplowed poorland
And the pine-woods roar like the surf.

Here the Roman lived on the wind-barren lonely,
Dark now and haunted by the moorland fowl;
None comes here now but the peewit only,
And moth-like death in the owl.

Beauty was here in on this beetle-droning downland;
The thought of a Caesar in the purple came
From the palace by the Tiber in the Roman townland
To this wind-swept hill with no name.

Lonely Beauty came here and was here in sadness,
Brave as a thought on the frontier of the mind,
In the camp of the wild upon the march of madness,
The bright-eyed Queen of the Blind.

Now where Beauty was are the wind-withered gorses,
Moaning like old men in the hill-wind's blast;
The flying sky is dark with running horses,
And the night is full of the past.

哲木斯・司梯芬斯（James Stephens）

風

風站了起來，一聲吶喊；
他在指尖上吹了個呼哨，就
踢得枯葉亂翻，
手掌把樹枝敲抖，

他就說他要殺啊，殺啊，殺啊；
看吧，他定會這麼做！定會這麼做！

一九五五年五月十二日下午七時

The Wind

The wind stood up and gave a shout.

He whistled on his fingers and

Kicked the withered leaves about
And thumped the branches with his hand.

And said he'd kill and kill and kill,
And so he will! And so he will!

祕密

我吃了一驚，因為在草間
一陣風爬過，竟說起
我昨天
心上的一件事──

一件我不了解的事
這風卻能知情；
我本來在我心裡
把牠埋得那麼深！

一九五五年六月十日夜十二時

The Secret

I was frightened, for a wind
Crept along the grass, to say
Something that was in my mind
Yesterday—

Something that I did not know
Could be found out by the wind;
I had buried it so low
In my mind!

晏珠・馬維爾（Andrew Marvell）

花園

1

人們徒然叫自己窘，
想贏取棕櫚，橡樹，和月桂；
他們在塵世不斷地辛苦，
成功的冠冕上只裝飾得幾片草木，
細小的綠葉一轉眼就枯凋，
有意地嘲笑著他們苦心的徒勞；
可是一切的花樹都簇擁做一團，
變織成恬靜底花環，

2

美麗的寧靜呵，我在這兒找到了你，
還找到了天真，你底可愛的姐妹！
我先前一直是弄錯了，
老是到擾擾的人群裡去把你尋找。
原來只有這片叢林裡低溼的地上，

你神聖的枝葉才會生長。
若比起你幽美的寂寞，
人事便只現得粗魯。

3
從來也不見任何桃紅和粉白
有這媚人的翠綠這般可愛。
熱戀的人們像熱烈般的冷酷，
竟把他們情人底名字刻上樹木。
唉，他們簡直不知道，或並沒在意，
諸樹底美超過了她底多少倍！

美麗的樹喲！若是我竟也要來把你底皮膚弄傷，
除了你自己的名字，別的是什麼也不會刻上。

4
當我們底熱情熱透了頂，
愛情就在這裡做最好的撤退。
神們追求人世不被長久的美，
也總是追到樹前為止。
亞坡羅想把達芙妮獵取，
只因她會變成桂花樹。
牧神潘因追逐著色倫克絲，
也不因她是女神而是蘆葦。

5

我底一生是多麼美麗輝煌，
成熟的蘋果落到頭上；
甜蜜的葡萄成串成球；
在我嘴裡擠出美酒；
還有甘露蟠桃是多麼鮮美，
自動地落到了我底手裡；
我邊走邊在瓜果中踉蹌，
花絆住了我，我就摔倒在草地上。

6

這時候心靈避開了轉少的享樂，
卻到牠沉思的快樂裡去深躲：
心靈好像清澈的海洋，
萬物都在裡面照出影像；
可是牠還超出了這些之外，
創造別的世界被造成的形象
消溶成綠色影子裡綠色的思想。

7

在這噴泉滑溜溜的腳旁，
或比在鋪滿青苔的果樹跟上，
我底靈魂拋開了肉體
飛進了茂盛的樹林裡：
像隻小鳥坐在枝上歌唱，

還梳理牠銀色的翅膀；
為了更遠的翱翔正待安排，
羽毛波動成繽紛的光彩。

8
這正是那個遠古的樂園，
男人在裡面還沒有伙伴：
住過這樣素潔可愛的境地，
別的助手哪裡再能相配！
可是在這裡作單獨的漫遊
實在是凡人所不能銷受：
在天堂裡獨個兒生活遊蕩，
那是雙重的天堂。

9
園丁底技巧真正熟練，
用花草做成了嶄新的鐘面；
太陽溫和地照耀在天空，
繞過這芬芳的黃道十二宮，
這時候，蜜蜂多麼勤勉，
像我們一樣把時間計較。
這般甜蜜而新鮮的光陰
除了用花草來稱怎麼稱得清！

The Garden

1

How vainly men themselves amaze
To win the Palm, the oak, or Bayes;
And their uncessant labors see
Crown'd from some single herb or tree,
Whose short and narrow verged shade
Does prudently their toil s upbraid;
While all flow'rs and all Trees do close
To weave the Garlands of repose.

2

Fair quiet, have I found thee here,
And Innocence thy Sister dear!
Mistaken long, I sought you then
In busy companies of men.
Your sacred Plants, if here below,
Only among the Plants will grow.
Society is all but rude,
To this delicious Solitude.

3

No white nor red was ever seen
So am'rous as this lovely green.

Fond Lovers, cruel as their flame,

Cut in these Trees their Mistress name.

Little, Alas, they know, or heed,

How far these Beauties Hers exceed!

Fair trees! where s'e'er your barks I wound,

No Name shall but your own be found.

4

When we have run our Passions heat,

Love hither makes his best retreat.

The gods, that mortal Beauty chase,

Still in a Tree did end their race.

Apollo hunted Daphne so,

Only that She might Laurel grow.

And Pan did after Syrinx speed,

Not as a Nymph, but for a Reed.

5

What wond'rous Life in this I lead!

Ripe Apples drop about my head;

The luscious clusters of the vine

Upon my Mouth do crush their Wine;

The nectarine, and curious peach,

Into my hands themselves do reach;

Stumbling on Melons, as I pass,

Insnar'd with Flow'rs, I fall on grass.

6

Meanwhile the Mind, from pleasure less,
Withdraws into its happiness:
The Mind, that Ocean where each kind
Does straight its own resemblance find;
Yet it creates, transcending these,
Far other Worlds, and other Seas;
Annihilating all that's made
To a green Thought in a green Shade.

7

Here at the Fountains sliding foot,
Or at some Fruit-trees mossy root,
Casting the body's vest aside,
My Soul into the boughs does glide:
There like a Bird it sits, and sings,
Then whets, and combs its silver wings;
And, till prepar'd for longer flight,
Waves in its Plumes the various light.

8

Such was that happy garden-state,
While man there walk'd without a mate:
After a place so pure, and sweet,
What other help could yet be meet!

But 'twas beyond a mortal's share
To wander solitary there:
Two paradises 'twere in one
To live in Paradise alone.

9
How well the skilful gardner drew
Of flow'rs and herbs this dial new;
Where from above the milder sun
Does through a fragrant zodiac run;
And, as it works, th' industrious bee
Computes its time as well as we.
How could such sweet and wholesome hours
Be reckon'd but with herbs and flow'rs!

給他撒嬌的情人

若是我們底世界和日子還夠多，
姑娘啊這怕羞倒也算不得罪過。
我們就會坐下來思量到哪兒去逛，
到哪兒去消磨這長長的戀愛的時光。
你去印度的恆河岸邊撿紅寶石；

我卻向英國的漢伯河潮水唉聲歎氣。
我會在洪水淹天門之前十年
就起心愛你；而你卻隨你底便
非到猶太人改信了教
絕不接受我這愛的感召。
我這富於生長力的愛情將生長泛濫，
長得比帝國還要大，也長得更慢。
一百年用來讚美你底眼睛，
來緊盯住你底眉心。
兩百年用來愛慕你每個乳房；
卻把三萬年用在其餘的東西上。
至少每一部分該消磨一個世代，
最後那一代是要把你底心來打開。
因為姑娘啊，你真值得這麼高貴的戀；
比這低俗的愛，我也絕不願。
但是在我背後我老是聽到
時光底飛車匆匆地接近了：
在我們面前那兒一直躺著
一片永恆大沙漠。
你底美將消失得毫無蹤影，
你大理石的墓窖裡，再也聽不到迴旋的歌聲；
於是蛀蟲就要來慢慢地咀嚼
那長期寶藏著的貞操；
你那吹毛求疵的自尊會變做灰塵，
而我底一切慾望也將成為餘燼。

墳墓固然僻靜又美好，
可是我想那兒絕不會有擁抱。
所以當著這年輕的色調
還像早晨的紅光和你底肌膚協調，
當著你底心靈還情願
讓每個毛孔呼出急迫的火焰，
這時我們能開心就該開心，
像一對多情的食肉的巖鷹，
寧可把我們底光陰一口吞掉，
卻不願慢慢地咀嚼而衰老。
讓我們把全部的精力和溫柔
一古腦兒捲成個圓球：
通過生命底鐵門檻
猛力撕裂我們底狂歡。
這樣，我們雖不能把太陽停掉，
卻會使牠飛跑。

一九五七年五月四日

To His Coy Mistress[1]

Had we but world enough and time,

This coyness, lady, were no crime.

We would sit down, and think which way

To walk, and pass our long love's day.

Thou by the Indian Ganges' side

Shouldst rubies find; I by the tide

Of Humber would complain. I would

Love you ten years before the flood,

And you should, if you please, refuse

Till the conversion of the Jews.

My vegetable love should grow

Vaster than empires and more slow;

An hundred years should go to praise

Thine eyes, and on thy forehead gaze;

Two hundred to adore each breast,

But thirty thousand to the rest;

An age at least to every part,

And the last age should show your heart.

For, lady, you deserve this state,

Nor would I love at lower rate.

---

[1]　【編者按】：此詩英文原文為編者所加，原書稿缺。

But at my back I always hear
Time's wingèd chariot hurrying near;
And yonder all before us lie
Deserts of vast eternity.
Thy beauty shall no more be found;
Nor, in thy marble vault, shall sound
My echoing song; then worms shall try
That long-preserved virginity,
And your quaint honour turn to dust,
And into ashes all my lust;
The grave's a fine and private place,
But none, I think, do there embrace.
    Now therefore, while the youthful hue
Sits on thy skin like morning dew,
And while thy willing soul transpires
At every pore with instant fires,
Now let us sport us while we may,
And now, like amorous birds of prey,
Rather at once our time devour
Than languish in his slow-chapped power.
Let us roll all our strength and all
Our sweetness up into one ball,
And tear our pleasures with rough strife
Through the iron gates of life:
Thus, though we cannot make our sun
Stand still, yet we will make him run.

桑塔雅納（Georgr Santayana）

你有什麼財富？

你有什麼財富可以當我是貧窮，
你有什麼安慰可以說我是憂愁？
告訴我什麼使你這般極端快樂：
難道你底世界是幸福，你底天堂可以寄托？
我期望著天堂，因為星星永遠閃爍，
還帶來像我們先人們有過得消息。
我找不到更徹底的懷疑能使我瘋狂，
我不需要更活潑的愛情來保持純潔。
對於我，那老的信心猶有如每天的飲食；
我祝福他們底希望，祝福他們救世的志氣。
我心裡還在想著他們所說的。
這靈魂底勇敢也正是我所喜悅的。
我和這死者是那麼親的親屬，
我滿意地走向那壘壘的墳墓。

桑塔雅納每次抒寫美學時都不忘記道德的價值，他底「十四行

詩」特別能做到語句熱情，感情深刻，而富於肯定的能力。他底這
種詩是古詩運用在現代的最好例子。

一九五三年六月五日

What Riches Have You That You Deem Me Poor

What riches have you that you deem me poor,
Or what large comfort that you call me sad?
Tell me what makes you so exceeding glad:
Is your earth happy or your heaven sure?
I hope for heaven, since the stars endure
And bring such tidings as our fathers had.
I know no deeper doubt to make me mad,
I need no brighter love to keep me pure.
To me the faiths of old are daily bread;
I bless their hope, I bless their will to save,
And my deep heart still meaneth what they said.
It makes me happy that the soul is brave,
And, being so much kinsman to the dead,
I walk contented to the peopled grave.

Santayana was always concerned with moral values even when he was writing about esthetics. His sonnets are particularly warm in phrase, deep in feeling, and richly affirmative in effect. They are among the best contemporary examples of the antique form.

——Louis Untermeyer

泰布（John Banister Tabb）

演化

從黃昏有陰影
便有了火花；
從浮雲有靜默，
便有了雲雀；
從深心有狂歡，
便有了劇痛；
從死亡有寒灰，
於是復活。

一九五三年五月二十七日

Evolution

Out of the dusk a shadow,

Then, a spark;

Out of the cloud a silence,

Then, a lark;

Out of the heart a rapture,

Then, a pain;

Out of the dead, cold ashes,

Life again.

莎蕾・狄詩德（Sara Teasdale）

一瞥

斯闕豐[1]在春天吻過我，
魯濱在秋天吻過我，
可是軻林只看了我一眼
從來就沒吻過我。

斯闕豐底吻在嘲笑中遺失了，
魯濱底吻在遊戲中遺失了，
可是軻林[2]眼睛底一吻
卻日夜在我心頭縈繞。

一九五三年七月十五日

---

[1] 斯闕豐（Strephone）是Sir Philip Sidney所著散文傳奇Arcadia (1590)中牧羊人底名字，他因失去了女郎Urania而非常悲傷。

[2] 在Edmund Spencer底長詩Shepheardes Calendar 及Colin Clout's Come Homr again中Colin Clout是個失戀的牧童。

The Look

Strephon kissed me in the spring,
Robin in the fall,
But Colin only looked at me
And never kissed at all.

Strephon's kiss was lost in jest,
Robin's lost in play,
But the kiss in Colin's eyes
Haunts me night and day.

忘了吧

忘掉它，像忘掉一朵花，
像忘了那發過黃金笑聲的火，
把它永遠永遠忘了吧，
年華這朋友真好，他會使我們蒼老。

要是有人問起，就說：
那再好久以前早已忘盡，

像忘了一朵花，一星火，
和那久已忘了的雪地上沉寂的腳步聲

聞一多詩集死水中〈忘掉她〉一詩顯然受了這詩的影響，為他
第五、六首詩：

忘掉她，像一朵忘掉的花！
年華那朋友真好，
他明天就教你老；
忘掉她，像一朵忘掉的花！

忘掉她，像一朵忘掉的花！
如果是有人要問，
就說沒有那個人；
忘掉她，像一朵忘掉的花！
（見全集第三冊，死水，頁14）

一九五三年六月十二夜

Let It Be Forgotten

Let it be forgotten, as a flower is forgotten,
Forgotten as a fire that once was singing gold.

Let it be forgotten forever and ever,
Time is a kind friend, he will make us old.

If anyone asks, say it was forgotten
Long and long ago,
As a flower, as a fire, as a hushed footfall
In a long-forgotten snow.

戀歌

你把笛鞋子穿在我腳上，
你給我美酒和麵包，
你喚我出來，到太陽和星星下來，
說全世界都是我的了。

唉，請把我腳上的鞋子脫去罷，
你簡直不懂你做了些什麼；
因為我整個世界早已在你懷抱裡，
我底太陽和星星就是你。

一九五六年十二月三十一日下午五時譯於20 Sumner Road, Cambridge, Mass

Song

You bound strong sandals on my feet,

You gave me bread and wine,

And bade me out, 'neath sun and stars,

For all the world was mine.

Oh take the sandals off my feet,

You know not what you do;

For all my world is in your arms,

My sun and stars are you.

莫憂（Harvey P. Moyer）

我爸爸是個社會主義的信徒

我爸爸是個社會主義的信徒，還有媽和我，
假如你願等一會兒，我要告訴你這是為什麼；
我相信你會明白了，一定也會看出這個奧妙，
都原做社會主義的信徒，還投我爸和我的票。

你知道這個世界多麼長多麼寬，好的東西真不少，
還有那麼多的人民，都想把事情辦好；
而且我們恰好都相同，都要吃飯穿衣和休息，
假如大家都是社會主義的信徒，大家就會平分一切。

可是現在煤油大王獨佔了油礦，銀行，和鐵路，
還有少數人佔有了全部的田土，
窮人們勞碌飢餓求職業，工作，工作，又工作，
把積來的財產都交給慵懶的闊人們去揮霍。

難道世上的爸爸都是大傻瓜？
要不然，怎麼肯把自己底東西都交給不生產的人們去花，

讓那少數的富豪過著舒服的生活，
而勞碌的工人們卻要受苦，挨窮，和沒落。

我時常奇怪，他們為什麼要那麼笨幹，
為了「罷工」，叫我們啼餓號寒；
要是他們都加入了社會主義樂園，只消四年或五年
大家都會變成這世界上偉大勞動陣營中富足的同伴。

因為只要想一想，就該明白這是多麼容易的道路，
一夥兒，創造我們所需要的，取得我們所創造的；
於是所有的孩子們，還有我們底爸和媽，都會同享幸福，
正如社會主義信徒所號召的。

所以爸爸就成了社會主義的信徒，還有媽和我們孩子們
我們要使所有的孩子們都富足和快樂，難道你不願麼？
我們孩子們需要好的食品好的家，漂亮的鞋子和衣服，難道你不要
麼？
所以我們都是社會主義的信徒；來吧，難道你不願做一個麼？

一九五一年四月二十八日，自社會主義之歌。

My Papa Is A Socialist

My papa is a Socialist, my mamma, too, and I, And if you'll wait a minute now, I'll tell the reason why; I'm sure that when you understand, you certainly will see, You'd better all be Socialists, and vote with pa and me.

You see this earth is long and wide, good things above, below, And there are lots of people, too, who want to make things go; Besides, we're all just quite alike, need food and clothes and rest, And if we all were Socialists, we all would share earth's best.

But now John D. owns all the oil, most banks, and railroads, too, And then a few own all the land, so what can poor folks do But tramp and starve and beg for jobs, and work and work and work? And all the wealth we make, but scraps, we give the wealthy shirk.

Now isn't every papa, most, the very biggest goose, To give away most all he makes to men who don't produce? So that a few rich families may all be living fine, While all we weary working folks must suffer, want, and pine.

And then they do such foolish things, I often wonder why They "strike" and lose their jobs, and let us freeze and starve and cry; When, if all joined the Socialists, in four years more or five We'd all be wealthy partners in the world's greatest working hive.

For if they'd stop to think, they'd see how easy 'twas to make, Together, all we'd want to have, and what we'd make, we'd take; So that the children, all alike, our papas, mammas, too, Would all enjoy earth's happiness, as Socialists want all to.

So papa is a Socialist, mamma, we children, too; We want to make all children rich and happy, too, don't you? Good food and homes, nice shoes and clothes, we children want, don't you? So all of us are Socialists; please, won't you be one too?

惠特曼（What Withman）

大閥斧歌

兵器，堂皇的，赤裸的，青蒼，
頭腦抽出自母底心腸，[1]
木的肉，鐵的骨，只一片嘴脣，一隻手臂膀，
灰藍色的葉子從赤熱中生長，
木柄是渺小的種子伸張，
休息在草中，休息在草上，
我依靠你，你也依靠在我身上！

---

[1] 【編者按】：此句原稿部分文字模糊，現由編者按英文原文與原書稿斟酌定稿。

Song of the Broad-Axe

Weapon shapely, naked, wan,

Head from the mother's bowels drawn,

Wooded flesh and metal bone, limb only one and lip only one,

Gray-blue leaf by red-heat grown, helve produced from a little seed sown,

Resting the grass amid and upon,

To be lean'd and to lean on.

斯賓德（Stephen Spender）

我不斷的想念

我不斷的想念那些真正偉大的人們，
他們從出生，就記住了靈魂底歷史，
那靈魂經過了光明之路，
在那兒，時間就是恒星，無盡而帶著歌聲。
他們可愛的雄心
是他們那還接觸著火焰的嘴脣
將訴說那整個裹在歌聲裡的心靈。
他們也從春天的枝條上儲藏
他們身上落下花朵般的欲望。

最寶貴的是：不要忘記
那鮮血底主要歡喜，
它從不老底春天流出。
衝破了在我們這地球之前的大千世界的巖石。
不要否認在這樸素的晨光中這血底快意，
和它那莊嚴的黃昏對愛的需求。

不要讓那人生道上的擁擠，用迷霧和嘈雜
逐漸悶塞了心靈底開花。

挨近著白雪，挨近著太陽，在那最高的原野裡
你看那波浪般起伏的綠草，
和招展的白雲旗幟，
和那傾聽著的天空裡低訴的風聲，
怎樣把這些名字撫慰。
這些名字屬於那一些為生命而奮鬥的人們，
他們心裡帶著火焰底中心。
他們出生自太陽，經過了短促的旅程又走向太陽，
在活潑的空中簽下了他們底光榮。

一九五三年六月一日夜

I Think Continually of Those

I think continually of those who were truly great.
Who, from the womb, remembered the soul's history
Through corridors of light where the hours are suns
Endless and singing. Whose lovely ambition
Was that their lips, still touched with fire,

Should tell of the Spirit clothed from head to foot in song.

And who hoarded from the Spring branches

The desires falling across their bodies like blossoms.

What is precious is never to forget

The essential delight of the blood drawn from ageless springs

Breaking through rocks in worlds before our earth.

Never to deny its pleasure in the morning simple light

Nor its grave evening demand for love.

Never to allow gradually the traffic to smother

With noise and fog the flowering of the spirit.

Near the snow, near the sun, in the highest fields

See how these names are feted by the waving grass

And by the streamers of white cloud

And whispers of wind in the listening sky.

The names of those who in their lives fought for life

Who wore at their hearts the fire's center.

Born of the sun they traveled a short while towards the sun,

And left the vivid air signed with their honor.

普希庚（Alexander Pushkin）

你拋棄了這異國

你拋棄了這異國
去尋找遙遠的故鄉；
離別時我怎禁得不流淚
當憂愁超過了限量？
我要用越來越冰冷的雙手
緊牽住你，也無話可說，
只求我們遠別的悲傷
永無了結。

但你在這緊抱和苦吻的當兒
忽然把嘴脣撇開，
叫我從這孤寂流亡的陰霾地方
到你那嶄新的國度裡來。
你說：「等我們再見時，
在無限蔚藍的天空下，
在橄欖樹的柔蔭裡，
嘴脣親著嘴脣，我再來安慰你。」

可是那兒喲，那兒的藍天已多麼透明，
岸邊的橄欖樹
在水上投著柔和的影子，
只你卻睡著再也不醒。
於今你底苦難和你底美
都埋在灰塵裡——
但我還等待著我們再見時
那蜜吻……我堅信你底誓言。

一九五七年十月二十六日下午一時譯於266A Harvard St., Cambridge, Mass

"Abandoning an Alien Country"

Abandoning an alien country,
You sought your distant native land;
How could I stop the tears at parting
When sorrow was beyond command?
With hands that momentary grew colder
I tried to hold you wordlessly
I begged that our farewells, our anguish,
Might be prolonged eternally.

But from the bitter lips and clinging
You tore away your lips; and from
The lonely land of exile
To a new land bade me come.
You said: when we are united,
Beneath a sky of endless blue
In the soft shadows of the olives,
Then, lip to lip, I'll solace you.

But yonder, where the blue is radiant,
And where the olives from the shore
Cast tender shadows on the waters,
You fell asleep to wake no more,
The funeral urn, alas, is holding
The beauty and your sorrow now,
But the sweet kiss of our reunion
I wait⋯ I hold you to your now.

湯木斯・俄爾夫（Thomas Wolfe）

深夜有聲音向我說

深夜有聲音向我說，
當殘年的蠟燭正在燃燒；
深夜有聲說過了，
告訴了我我將死去，但我不知將在何處。

他說：
「你將喪失你所知的大地，為了更大的智慧；
你將喪失你所有的生命，為了更大的生命；
你將訣別你所愛的朋友們，為了更大的愛情；
去尋找一塊國土比家更溫暖，比大地更大──」

「在那兒地球底柱奠基，
現世底良知對它負責──
那兒有風吹，有河流。」

一九五五年七月八日下午四時譯於密西根大學研究院閱鑒定

Something Has Spoken To Me In The Night

Something has spoken to me in the night,

Burning the tapers of the waning year;

Something has spoken in the night,

And told me I shall die, I know not where.

Saying:

"To lose the earth you know, for greater knowing;

To lose the life you have, for greater life;

To leave the friends you loved, for greater loving;

To find a land more kind than home, more larger than earth—

Whereon the pillars of this earth are founded,

Toward which the conscience of the world is tending—

A wind is rising, and the rivers flow."

華滋華斯（William Wordsworth）

我們是七個

一個天真爛漫的孩子，
輕輕地呼吸，
她覺得活力充滿了四肢，
哪裡會知道什麼是死？

我遇見了一位住鄉村小姑娘：
她說：她是八歲年紀；
她底頭髮堆滿在頭上，
捲曲而濃密。

她有鄉村和山林的風度，
她有天然放蕩的裝束，
她眼睛長得美麗，美麗無邊，
──她底美討得我喜歡。

「小姑娘，你有多少
兄弟和姐妹？」
她望著我楞了一楞，答道：
「多少位麼？一共七位。」

「他們在什麼地方？請你告訴我。」
她答道：「我們是七個：
兩個住在康城地方，還有兩個在海上。

另外兩個躺在教堂底墳地，
一個是我姐姐，一個是我弟弟；
在那墳場邊的莊上，
我和我媽就住在他們近旁。」

「你說你們有兩個住在康城地方，
還有兩個在海上，
可是你們還是七位！
好姑娘，告訴我，這怎麼對？」

於是這小姑娘回答：
「我們是七個男孩和女孩。
我們有兩個躺在那教堂墳場地樹下。」

「你到處飛跑，我底小姑娘，
因為你底小腿兒還有知覺，

要是有兩位躺在墳場上，
那你們就只有五個。」

「他們在墳上一片綠，他們並沒有消失，」
這小姑娘趕快解釋，
「從我媽底門口走十二步多，
他們並排地躺著。

我時常在那兒織我底長襪，
我也在那兒鑲我底手帕；
我還坐在那個墳地，
唱個歌給他們聽。

先生，當天氣晴朗的時候，
往往在太陽落山之後，
我總帶著我底小杯盤，
到那兒去吃晚餐。

第一個死去的是我姐姐哲因，
她躺著在床上呻吟，
直呻吟到上帝解脫了她底痛苦；
於是她就永別而去。

因此她就給安放在教堂底墳地，
只要那草地一乾，

我就常和我弟弟約翰
圍著她底墳墓遊戲。

當白雪鋪滿了地面，
我能溜跑得多麼好玩，
可是弟弟卻被迫長眠，
他就躺在她底旁邊。」

我說：「如果他們兩位已到了天上，
那麼現在你們一共還有幾個？」

這小姑娘回答得那麼快，
「老先生啊！我們是七個。」

「可是他們已經死了。那兩位已經死了！
他們底靈魂早已上了天了！」
這些話終歸白說，
因為這小姑娘總會把她底心願固執著，
永遠地說：「不，我們是七個！」

一九五一年九月十三日夜三時

We Are Seven

—A Simple Child,
That lightly draws its breath,
And feels its life in every limb,
What should it know of death?

I met a little cottage Girl:
She was eight years old, she said;
Her hair was thick with many a curl
That clustered round her head.

She had a rustic, woodland air,
And she was wildly clad:
Her eyes were fair, and very fair;
—Her beauty made me glad.

"Sisters and brothers, little Maid,
How many may you be?"
"How many? Seven in all," she said
And wondering looked at me.

"And where are they? I pray you tell."
She answered, "Seven are we;

And two of us at Conway dwell,
And two are gone to sea."

"Two of us in the church-yard lie,
My sister and my brother;
And, in the church-yard cottage, I
Dwell near them with my mother."

"You say that two at Conway dwell,
And two are gone to sea,
Yet ye are seven!—I pray you tell,
Sweet Maid, how this may be."

Then did the little Maid reply,
"Seven boys and girls are we;
Two of us in the church-yard lie,
Beneath the church-yard tree."

"You run above, my little Maid,
Your limbs they are alive;
If two are in the church-yard laid,
Then ye are only five."

"Their graves are green, they may be seen,"
The little Maid replied,

"Twelve steps or more from my mother's door,
And they are side by side."

"My stockings there I often knit,
My kerchief there I hem;
And there upon the ground I sit,
And sing a song to them. "

"And often after sun-set, Sir,
When it is light and fair,
I take my little porringer,
And eat my supper there. "

"The first that died was sister Jane;
In bed she moaning lay,
Till God released her of her pain;
And then she went away."

"So in the church-yard she was laid;
And, when the grass was dry,
Together round her grave we played,
My brother John and I. "

"And when the ground was white with snow,
And I could run and slide,

My brother John was forced to go,
And he lies by her side. ”

“How many are you, then,” said I,
“If they two are in heaven?”
Quick was the little Maid's reply,
“O Master! we are seven.”

“But they are dead; those two are dead!
Their spirits are in heaven!”
'Twas throwing words away; for still
The little Maid would have her will,
And said, “Nay, we are seven!”

給一隻蝴蝶

挨近我，你不要飛開！
讓我多看你一會兒
從你——我童年的史家，
我發現了無窮的對話
飄近我，不要飛開呀！
死去了的光陰會讓你復活：

你這愉快的小東西啊！
你帶到我心中一個嚴肅的幻影，
——我父親的家庭！

啊，多麼快樂，快樂的光陰！
我和我妹妹愛茉林，
在童年時光，
一道去捉蝴蝶！
我就像個獵人
跑去打獵：——
蹦蹦跳跳地踏遍了叢林；
可是她，上帝愛她吧，卻生怕
抖掉蝴蝶翅膀上的彩粉。

一九五五年七月十四日

To A Butterfly

Stay near me—do not take thy flight!
A little longer stay in sight!
Much converse do I find in thee,
Historian of my infancy!

Float near me; do not yet depart!

Dead times revive in thee:

Thou bring'st, gay creature as thou art!

A solemn image to my heart,

My father's family!

Oh! pleasant, pleasant were the days,

The time, when, in our childish plays,

My sister Emmeline and I

Together chased the butterfly!

A very hunter did I rush

Upon the prey:—with leaps and springs

I followed on from brake to bush;

But she, God love her, feared to brush

The dust from off its wings.

霓虹

當我看見一道霓虹在天上，

我底心就跳：

我初生時曾這樣；

而今已成年，還是這樣；

等我年老，依然會這樣，

否則不如讓我死去！

孩子是成年底父親；

我還可願望自然神

把我一生的日子緊結在一處。

一九五一年九月八日夜十二時譯於笨比明寓所

"My heart leaps up when I behold"

My heart leaps up when I behold

A rainbow in the sky :

So was it when my life began ;

So is it now I am a man ;

So be it when I shall grow old,

Or let me die ! The Child is father of the Man ;

And I could wish my days to be

Bound each to each by natural piety.

露茜・孤蕾

我時常聽說到露茜・孤蕾：
當我走過那片荒地，
黎明中，我偶然看到
那寂寞的孩子。

露茜沒有伴侶，也沒有知心，
她住在一個廣闊的荒境，
──這是生長在「人的門戶」邊，
唯一可愛的生命。

可是你也許會覷見小鹿在遊玩，
綠地上有野兔出現；
只是那露茜可愛的面龐，
再也不能看見。

「今夜會有風景到來──
你該去鎮上，我底小乖，
你還得帶一個燈籠
去照著你媽從雪地回來。」

「爸啊！我會很高興去這一趟：
還是下午辰光──

教堂底鐘纔敲了兩下，
月亮也剛剛昇上！」

這時那父親把鐮刀舞動，
去砍劈乾柴一篷，
當他正辛勤地工作——
露茜就拿了燈籠在手中。

她快樂得像山上的小鹿：
當無數雜亂的腳步，
踢散了路上的雪花，
像白煙一般飛舞。

那過早的風暴來得不提防：
露茜上上下下地流浪；
她爬過了無數山頭，
終不曾走到鎮上。

她可憐的爸媽在那個通宵，
到處高叫著去尋找，
但是沒有音響或蹤跡
可給他們一點指導。

黎明時，他們還在深山裡，
向望得見那一片荒地；

從那兒他們看見了一道木橋，
離他們底門口不到半里。

他們哭了──在回家路上，痛哭失聲，
「我們一夥兒只有在天堂再相親」
──當那母親在雪地上走過時，
卻發現了露茜底腳印。

於是他們從那陡峻的山上，
走下來追蹤那小小的足跡底方向，
通過那破倒的山楂樹籬笆，
沿著那漫長的石頭牆。

當他們走過一片平原：
那足跡還是依然；
他們追溯著，
直尋到他們來時經過的那道橋邊。

他們沿那積雪的河岸走過，
跟隨著那些腳印，一個又一個，
到了那木板橋底中央，
就再也找不著！

──可是直到今天還有人堅持，
她依然是一個活著的孩子；

你還可看見這可愛的露茜
在這淒涼的荒野裡。

她奔波在險峻和平坦的地方，
從來不回頭張望，
還唱著一隻寂寞的歌
在淒風飄蕩。

一九五一年九月十五日夜三時於密大

Lucy Gray; or, Solitude

Oft I had heard of Lucy Gray:

And, when I crossed the wild,

I chanced to see at break of day

The solitary child.

No mate, no comrade Lucy knew;

She dwelt on a wide moor,

—The sweetest thing that ever grew

Beside a human door!

You yet may spy the fawn at play,

The hare upon the green;

But the sweet face of Lucy Gray

Will never more be seen.

To-night will be a stormy night—

You to the town must go;

And take a lantern, Child, to light

Your mother through the snow.

That, Father! will I gladly do:

'T is scarcely afternoon—

The minster-clock has just struck two,

And yonder is the moon!

At this the Father raised his hook,

And snapped a fagot-band;

He plied his work;—and Lucy took

The lantern in her hand.

Not blither is the mountain roe:

With many a wanton stroke

Her feet disperse the powdery snow,

That rises up like smoke.

The storm came on before its time:

She wandered up and down;

And many a hill did Lucy climb:

But never reached the town.

The wretched parents all that night

Went shouting far and wide;

But there was neither sound nor sight

To serve them for a guide.

At day-break on a hill they stood

That overlooked the moor;

And thence they saw the bridge of wood,

A furlong from their door.

They wept—and, turning homeward, cried,

In Heaven we all shall meet;

—When in the snow the mother spied

The print of Lucy's feet.

Then downwards from the steep hill's edge

They tracked the footmarks small;

And through the broken hawthorn hedge,

And by the long stone-wall;

And then an open field they crossed:

The marks were still the same;

They tracked them on, nor ever lost;

And to the bridge they came.

They followed from the snowy bank

Those footmarks, one by one,

Into the middle of the plank;

And further there were none!

—Yet some maintain that to this day

She is a living child;

That you may see sweet Lucy Gray

Upon the lonesome wild.

O'er rough and smooth she trips along,

And never looks behind;

And sings a solitary song

That whistles in the wind.

愛德孟・華樓（Edmund Waller）

詠羅帶

牠纏著她織巧的腰，
我愉快的心靈也纏在一道：
沒有個國王不寧願拋棄皇冠，
只要能像牠那般擁抱。

這是我天堂最遠的角落，
這柵欄關著那可愛的小鹿：
我底悲歡，希望，和愛情
全在這圈兒裡打滾。

只是一塊小小的園地！
卻住著一切美好的物件：
只要把牠繞著的東西給我，
我情願拿全世界來交換。

一九五六年十一月十四日夜二時譯於20 Sumner Road, Cambridge, Mass

On a Girdle

That which her slender waist confined
Shall now my joyful temples bind:
No monarch but would give his crown
His arms might do what this has done.

It was my Heaven's extremest sphere.
The pale which held that lovely deer:
My joy, my grief, my hope, my love,
Did all within this circle move.

A narrow compass! and yet there
Dwelt all that 's good, and all that 's fair:
Give me but what this ribband bound,
Take all the rest the sun goes round.

愛德納・密勒
（Edna St. Vincent Millay）

別憐恤我

別憐恤我只為了白天的光輝
在黃昏的時候就要消失；
別憐恤我只因為年華如水
田野和叢林裡美已絕跡；
別為了月亮蒼白就對我憐恤；
也別為了潮水流回了海洋；
更別因為青年的戀火轉瞬就要熄滅，
而你再也不把我放在心上。

我早就領會了：愛情不過是
西風摧折中繽紛的花瓣；
不過是蹂躪著崩岸的潮水
把風暴裡堆積的船骸吹散。
只憐恤我：這痴心覺悟得太慢，
偉愛智慧是那麼敏感。

一九五五年六月二十八日夜九時，六月二十九日修改。

Pity Me Not

Pity me not because the light of day
At close of day no longer walks the sky;
Pity me not for beauties passed away
From field and thicket as the year goes by;
Pity me not the waning of the moon,
Nor that the ebbing tide goes out to sea,
Nor that a man's desire is hushed so soon,
And you no longer look with love on me.

This have I known always; love is no more
Than the wide blossom which the wind assails,
Than the great tide that treads the shifting shore,
Strewing fresh wreckage gathered in the gales.
Pity me that the heart is slow to learn
What the swift mind beholds at every turn.

我吻過了什麼嘴脣

我忘了我吻過了什麼嘴脣，
在什麼地方，為什麼原因，

什麼樣的臂膀擁抱過我直到早晨；

可是今夜的雨卻充滿了幽靈，

在玻璃上輕敲，微歎，聽候著回音；

它激起了我心中一陣隱痛，

為了那些已經給遺忘了的人們

再也不會在午夜來輕輕呼喚，和我就近。

就這樣，冬天裡站著那株孤零的樹，

也不知是什麼鳥群一一地飛散過，

只覺得那樹枝比以前更沉默了：

我說不清是什麼樣的愛情來過又失去了；

只知道夏天在我心裡歌唱過一遭，

而今是再也不歌唱了。

一九五四年十月

What Lips My Lips Have Kissed

What lips my lips have kissed, and where, and why,

I have forgotten, and what arms have lain

Under my head till morning; but the rain

Is full of ghosts tonight, that tap and sigh

Upon the glass and listen for replay;

And in my heart there stirs a quiet pain

For unremembered lads that not again

Will turn to me at midnight with a cry.

Thus in the winter stands the lonely tree,

Nor knows what birds have vanished one by one,

Yet knows its boughs more silent than before:

I cannot say what loves have come and gone;

I only know that summer sang in me

A little while, that in me sings no more.

念黃海漁夫，鮑琴

他哪裡去了，
穿著帶蒜氣的髒汗衫，
黃昏時搖著舢板回家——
竹桅上掛著褶皺的紅帆；

他哪裡去了呢？
我將用愛戀和讚美
來終身紀念他，
只因他曾用一枝中國笛

為我吹過一支小曲。
從那時起我曾憂傷過；
曾流浪到多少城市，身無長物，只帶著這曲歌，──
我多麼珍重他呵，就是餓死也不肯便賣掉。

他哪裡去了呢？
為了他，我永遠在心裡
帶著這愛戀和讚美！

一九五六年十二月十一日夜一時譯於20 Sumner Road, Cambridge, Mass

　　這詩原載於一九二八年出版的《雪裡的雄鹿》。密勒女士早年
曾到過東方。

For Pao-Chin,
A Boatman On The Yellow Sea

Where is he now, in his soiled shirt reeking of garlic,
Sculling his sampan home, and night approaching fast—
The red sail hanging wrinkled on the bamboo mast;

Where is he now, I shall remember my whole life long

With love and praise, for the sake of a small song

Played on a Chinese flute?

I have been said;

I have been in cities where the song was all I had,—

A treasure never to be bartered by the hungry days.

Where is he now, for whom a carry in my heart

This love, this praise?

From The Buck in the Snow (1928).

愛德溫・馬克漢謨
（Edwin Markham）

你底眼淚

我不敢要求整個的你：
我只要求你底一部分
當跳舞的人們都離開了舞廳，
請帶給我──你劇痛的心。

給別的朋友們你快樂的臉龐，
和多年來的笑。
我卻來懇求更深的情意──
請帶給我你底眼淚。

一九五三年十二月二日夜一時半

Your Tears

I dare not ask your very all:

I only ask a part.

Bring me—when dancers leave the hall—

Your aching heart.

Give other friends your lighted face,

The laughter of the years:

I come to crave a greater grace—

Bring me your tears!

倚鋤人
——馬格觀賞米勒（Jean F. Millet）
著作世界馳名的油畫「倚鋤人」後

被千百年的重量壓彎了腰

他倚著鋤頭向地面瞧，

臉上堆滿古往今來的空虛，

背負起世界底義務。

是誰使他對狂歡與絕望都麻木，

成了一種不知悲哀也從不希望的動物，

一個魯鈍暈呆的，耕牛底弟兄？

是誰鬆開，拉下了這粗野的下顎？

誰底手掃斜了他底眉峰？

誰底呼吸吹熄了他心中的光？

難道這就是上帝造成的東西

造了他還給他海洋和陸地去統治；

去為了權利而追溯星星和搜索天堂；

去感覺「永恆」底情熱？

難道這就是造物者底夢？

他創造了星球還在遠古的頂點替牠們畫定了路。

下窮地獄的洞底，直到深淵，

從來沒有比這更可怕的形象——

比這更喋喋不休地被世上盲目的貪婪詛咒——

沒有比這更有靈魂底象徵和凶兆——

沒有比這對宇宙更填滿危機。

在他和天使們之間有著多麼寬的深淵！

柏拉圖和「七姐妹星」底旋轉[1]

與勞動齒輪下的奴隸有什麼相干？

---

[1] 「七姐妹星」，據希臘神話，是阿地拉斯（Atlas）底七個女兒所變成的七顆星。紀元前三世紀左右，希臘亞歷山大城底七位名詩人被叫做「七姐妹星」。第十六紀中，英、法國七詩人亦自稱「七姐妹星」詩人，提倡古典文學及法文底典麗堂皇，影響很大。在俄國十九世紀普希金及索蒙託夫也有此稱。二十世紀時，法國仍有不少詩人被稱作「七姐妹星」詩人。

陽光白雪的歌聲激越遠揚，
黎明底罅隙，薔薇底紅暈，與他有什麼相干？
一切受罪的世代通過這些恐怖的形像現形；
時間底悲劇存在這痛楚的屈身；
通過這些恐怖的形像，人類遭受了欺騙，
被搶劫了，被污辱了，被剝奪了繼承權，
就對創造世界的「權利」作抗議的吶喊。
這抗議也就是預言。

世界的主子們，帝王們，和統治者們啊，
這就是你們獻給上帝的親手製造品麼，——
這怪物般的，扭歪了的，消滅靈魂的製造品麼？
你們要怎樣整理這形像；
變回牠蓬勃的面貌和光；
在牠裡面重建音樂和夢想；
你們怎麼辯護這恒古以來的異名，
奸邪的虐待，和不可救藥的災難殃？

世界的主子們，帝王們，和統治者們啊，
後世將怎樣來把這個「人」結算？
怎樣回答那時候他殘酷的問題
當革命的旋風把全世界震撼？
牠對一切的王國和君主將怎麼辦
對那些製造這形像的人們將怎麼辦——

當這緘口的恐怖者沉默了千百年後
要起來給這世界作最後的裁判？

一九五五年六月二十九日上午十一時

　　「倚鋤人」是古今來最充滿義憤的，表現社會抗議精神的一首
詩。當十九世紀末葉，社會意識正在覺醒，貴族和資本家之間競爭
加劇，勞動者慘遭犧牲。馬克漢謨這位出生於美國奧內岡州，長大
於加利佛尼亞州的，沉默的教育工作者，從法國畫家米勒一幅油畫
上看到一個形容勞瘁的慧夫彎著身子倚在鋤頭上的形象，大受感
動，就把他當作一切勞動者的象徵，寫了這首詩，於十九世紀末的
最後一年（一八九九年）在舊金山的《考驗者》（Examiner）報上
發表。這詩一發表後來，非常成功，立刻引起了社會的注意，被輾
轉傳誦於世界各國。他把握了當時正需要表現的社會抗議的熱情，
因此喜被稱讚作「今後一千年間戰鬥的召喚。」陳勒（John Vance
Cheney, 1848-1922）曾用同題寫詩作答，用讚美勞動代表了抗議。
沒有馬氏原作那麼動人。

The Man with a Hoe

Bowed by the weight of centuries he leans
Upon his hoe and gazes on the ground,

The emptiness of ages in his face,

And on his back, the burden of the world.

Who made him dead to rapture and despair,

A thing that grieves not and that never hopes,

Stolid and stunned, a brother to the ox?

Who loosened and let down this brutal jaw?

Whose was the hand that slanted back this brow?

Whose breath blew out the light within this brain?

Is this the Thing the Lord God made and gave

To have dominion over sea and land;

To trace the stars and search the heavens for power;

To feel the passion of Eternity?

Is this the dream He dreamed who shaped the suns

And marked their ways upon the ancient deep?

Down all the caverns of Hell to their last gulf

There is no shape more terrible than this—

More tongued with cries against the world's blind greed—

More filled with signs and portents for the soul—

More packed with danger to the universe.

What gulfs between him and the seraphim!

Slave of the wheel of labor, what to him

Are Plato and the swing of the Pleiades?

What the long reaches of the peaks of song,

The rift of dawn, the reddening of the rose?

Through this dread shape the suffering ages look;

Time's tragedy is in that aching stoop;

Through this dread shape humanity betrayed,

Plundered, profaned and disinherited,

Cries protest to the Powers that made the world,

A protest that is also prophecy.

O masters, lords and rulers in all lands,

Is this the handiwork you give to God,

This monstrous thing distorted and soul-quenched?

How will you ever straighten up this shape;

Touch it again with immortality;

Give back the upward looking and the light;

Rebuild in it the music and the dream;

Make right the immemorial infamies,

Perfidious wrongs, immedicable woes?

O masters, lords and rulers in all lands,

How will the future reckon with this Man?

How answer his brute question in that hour

When whirlwinds of rebellion shake all shores?

How will it be with kingdoms and with kings—

With those who shaped him to the thing he is—

When this dumb Terror shall rise to judge the world,

After the silence of the centuries?

愛彌麗・狄更生（Emily Dickinson）

小陽春

這些日子裡鳥兒要回來，
可是只有少數，
只一兩隻飛來作一次回顧。

這些日子裡天空要披上
六月底舊偽裝——
一個灰暗而鮮豔的錯誤。

啊，虛飾不能把蜜蜂騙住，
你底花言巧語
卻幾乎誘我相信，

直到那一堆堆的種子作了證據，
還有，從那轉變了的空中，輕輕地，匆匆地，
飄下了一片羞怯的葉兒，我纔覺悟！

夏天的祭禮啊，
請容許一個孩子來參加，
來分享你神聖的幟號，
來分吃你的麵色，
來嘗嘗你不朽的酒餚！

一九五三年七月二十八日夜

Indian Summer

These are the days when birds come back,
A very few, a bird or two,
To take a backward look.
These are the days when skies put on
The old, old sophistries of June,—
A blue and gold mistake.

Oh, fraud that cannot cheat the bee,
Almost thy plausibility
Induces my belief,

Till ranks of seeds their witness bear,
And softly through the altered air
Hurries a timid leaf!

Oh, sacrament of summer days,
Oh, last communion in the haze,
Permit a child to join,

Thy sacred emblems to partake,
Thy consecrated bread to break,
Taste thine immortal wine!

因為我不能等待死神

因為我不能去找死神，
死神好心地來找我，
馬車裡只載著我們
和那位「永生」。

我們慢慢兒趕著車，他知道不用忙，
我也把勞作撇開了，

還把閒暇撇開了，
都為了他底慇懃。

我們經過了一個學堂
孩子們在那兒玩，扭做一團；
我們經過了禾黍油油的田園，
還經過了落山的太陽。

我們在一個房屋前面休息，
這房屋好像是地面底隆起；
屋頂迷茫幾乎看不見，
飛簷只是座岡巒。

從那時起已是好幾個世紀了；
可是我們都覺得比那一天還短促，
那一天，我初次擔心
馬頭是向著永恆。

一九五五年六月二十四日下午四時

Because I Could Not Stop for Death

Because I could not stop for Death,
He kindly stopped for me;
The carriage held but just ourselves
And Immortality.

We slowly drove, he knew no haste,
And I had put away
My labor, and my leisure too,
For his civility.

We passed the school where children played,
Their lessons scarcely done;
We passed the fields of gazing grain,
We passed the setting sun.

We paused before a house that seemed
A swelling of the ground;
The roof was scarcely visible,
The cornice but a mound.

Since then 't is centuries; but each
Feels shorter than the day

I first surmised the horses' heads
Were toward eternity.

我為美而死

我為美而死了，
可是我很少在墳裡轉變，
另一個人卻是為了真理而死，
就躺在一旁邊。

他問我為什麼而死去？
我回答說：「為了美」，
他說「他是為了真理」，
他還說：「我們是二而一」。

於是我們像親戚相逢在夜裡，
我們隔著房子交談，
談到直讓青苔封著了我們的嘴脣，
也淹沒了我們的姓名。

I Died for Beauty

I died for beauty, but was scarce
Adjusted in the tomb,
When one who died for truth was lain
In an adjoining room.
He questioned softly why I failed?
"For beauty," I replied.
"And I for truth,—the two are one;
We brethren are," he said.
And so, as kinsmen met a night,
We talked between the rooms.
Until the moss had reached our lips,
And covered up our names.

愛彌麗·葡朗特（Emily Bronte）

最後的詩行

我底靈魂不膽怯，
在這風暴擾亂的世界裡它不戰慄：
我看到了天堂光輝在照耀，
信心也在照耀，說我不受恐怖的威脅。

啊，我心中的上帝，
你全能的，用在的神！
生命──在我心中寧靜，
這不死的生命也像我從你而有偉力！

成千的教條都是空的，
雖然感動過人們底心，卻肯定是空的；
像枯萎了的亂草，
或者像茫茫大海中閒散的水泡。

這些教條不能引起個人底懷疑，
由於你底無限，他是那麼肯定，
他在那堅固的不朽之巖的旁邊
安安穩穩地把船兒下了碇。

你底精神用廣大懷抱的愛
鼓舞了無數永恆的年代，
它散布和彌漫在空中，
還變化，忍耐，溶解，創造，和繁榮。

雖然世界和人類都消滅了，
星球和宇宙也完結了，
只剩下一個孤另的你，
這一切生存還存在於你。

這兒『死亡』沒有地位，
原子也不能把真空造成：
你──你就是「存在」和「生命」，
無論你是什麼你都不會給摧毀。

一九五三年六月六日夜

Last Lines

No coward soul is mine,

No trembler in the world's storm-troubled sphere:

I see Heaven's glories shine,

And faith shines equal, arming me from fear.

O God within my breast,

Almighty, ever-present Deity!

Life—that in me has rest,

As I—undying Life—have power in thee!

Vain are the thousand creeds

That move men's hearts: unutterably vain;

Worthless as withered weeds,

Or idlest froth amid the boundless main,

To waken doubt in one

Holding so fast by thine infinity;

So surely anchored on

The stedfast rock of immortality.

With wide-embracing love

Thy spirit animates eternal years,

Pervades and broods above,

Changes, sustains, dissolves, creates, and rears.

Though earth and man were gone,

And suns and universes ceased to be,

And Thou were left alone,

Every existence would exist in Thee.

There is not room for Death,

Nor atom that his might could render void:

Thou—THOU art Being and Breath,

And what THOU art may never be destroyed.

葉芝（William Butler Yeats）

我底書所去的地方

我說的每一句話，
和寫的每一個字，
一定會不倦地展翅，
也不停地飛，
直飛到你憂鬱的心兒所在，
還向你歌唱，等夜深到來，
在那水流，濤湧，
和星光燦爛的境界之外。

一九五二年三月二十五日夜譯於安市

Where My Books Go

All the words that I utter,

And all the words that I write,

Must spread out their wings untiring,

And never rest in their flight,

Till they come where your sad, sad heart is,

And sing to you in the night,

Beyond where the waters are moving,

Storm-darken'd or starry bright.

他願有天上的錦繡

若是我有天上的錦繡，

上面鑲著金光和銀光，是深暗的，淺灰的，天藍的錦繡，

像午夜，像黃昏，也像陽光。

我願把牠鋪在你底腳下：

但是貧窮的我呀，我只有夢想；

我已把我底夢鋪在你底腳下；

請輕輕地踩吧，因為你踩在我底夢上。

一九五三年三月十三日夜譯於安市，譯文用韻方式大致和原作相同。

He Wishes For The Cloths Of Heaven[1]

Had I the heavens' embroidered cloths,
Enwrought with golden and silver light,
The blue and the dim and the dark cloths
Of night and light and the half-light,
I would spread the cloths under your feet:
But I, being poor, have only my dreams;
I have spread my dreams under your feet;
Tread softly because you tread on my dreams.

玫瑰樹

「話兒說得輕輕的呀，」
丕爾斯對康納利說，
「也許是幾句政客底官話
就把我們底玫瑰樹凋謝；
也許只由於海外吹來了
一陣暴風吧！」

---

[1] 【編者按】：此詩英文原文為編者所加，原書稿缺。

「現在只好來澆些水，」
康納利這麼答應，
「好叫綠葉兒再生，
還長得一團茂盛，
從發芽到開花，

The Rose Tree

'O words ale lightly spoken,'
Said Pearse to Connolly,
'Maybe a breath of politic words
Has withered our Rose Tree;
Or maybe but a wind that blows
Acrose the bitter sea.'

'It needs to be but watered,'
James Connolly replied,
'To make the green come out again
And spread on every side,
And shake the blossom from the bud
To be the garden's pride.'

'But where can we draw water,'
Said Pearse to Connolly,
'When all the walls are parched away?
O plain as plain can be
There's nothing but our own red blood
Can make a right Rose Tree.'

政治

「在我們這個時代裡人底命運只有跟政治的觀點出發才有意義。」
——Thomas Mann 湯木斯・曼

那女郎正亭亭玉立在那裡，
我怎麼能集中注意力
到羅馬的，俄國的，
或西班牙的政治呢？
可是這兒有個漫遊者，
他深知他自己永沒的一切，
這兒還有個政客
學經博覽群書，深謀遠慮，
他們說的戰爭和戰爭的警報，
也許都是真的，

但是啊，要是我再年輕了
又擁抱著她啊！

一九五五年五月二十一日下午二時半

Politics

"In our time the deitiny of man presents its meaning in political terms."

——Thomas Mann

How can I, that girl standing there,
My attention fix
On Roman or on Russian
Or on Spanish politics?
Yet here's a travelled man that knows
What he talks about,
And there's a politician
That has read and thought,
And maybe what they say is true
Of war and war's alarms,
But O that I were young again
And held her in my arms!

靜姑娘

「靜姑娘」哪兒去了？
她頭上裹著帕兒多麼深紅。
那驚醒過星星的風
還在我熱血裡吹送。
她起身離別的當兒，
我怎麼能無動於衷？
現在那喚起過閃電的話句
還在我心中激動。

一九五二年三月二十五日夜

Maid Quiet

Where has Maid Quiet gone to,
Nodding her russet hood?
The winds that awakened the stars
Are blowing through my blood.
O how could I be so calm
When she rose up to depart?

Now words that called up the lightning

Are hurtling through my heart.

瑪德林·艾欒（Madeleine Aaron）

量衣蟲（尺蠖——愛爾蘭的就送信）

天真的薛娜只有四歲，
帶著笑容和新奇，
正在看一件東西在她小手膀上往下爬，
她一點也不害怕。

她附近的玩伴們卻突然起了驚慌，
都跪到了她底身旁。
難道她已經著了魔？
為什麼不哭，連一聲也不做？

十隻眼睛一齊往下瞧；
五個小腦袋可怕地掉了又掉。
那年紀大一點的卻大都著了急
「它在量你底屍衣！」
「你馬上就要眼睛緊閉，
在白綾般的棺材裡安睡，

再也不能醒來和我們一道
玩「捉迷藏」和「烤麵包」的遊戲了……

薛娜像一隻傾聽的小鳥，
細味著這每一句話。
她張開星星般的眼睛說道：
來，我們就來玩「我死去了」這遊戲吧！

一九五三年六月三十日夜譯於Machigan Union

Measuring Worm
(Old Irish Superstition)

Sheila, four and innocent,
In her world of wonderment,
Watched with smiles, and not alarm,
Something creeping down her arm.

All her playmates who were near
Ran to her in sudden fear.
Was she charmed? She did not call
Or make any sound at all.

Ten round eyes looked down to see;
Five small heads shook awesomely.
Then the elder spoke aloud:
"It is measuring your shroud!"

"You will sleep, with eyelids tight,
In a box all satin white,
And will not wake up to play
Hiding-and-seek or baking day..."

Eager as a listening bird,
Sheila's ears drank every word.
Lifting starry eyes, she said:
"Come, let's play that I am dead!"

福勞斯特（Robert Frost）

火與冰

有人說世界會毀滅在火裡；
有人說會在冰裡。
從我對慾望的經驗看來
我贊成說在火裡。
可是牠如果必須毀滅兩次，
我想我知道了夠多的憎恨，
這使我相信
冰也是偉大而充分猛烈
可以把這世界毀滅。

一九五三年六月二十二日

Fire And Ice

Some say the world will end in fire,
Some say in ice.
From what I've tasted of desire
I hold with those who favor fire.
But if it had to perish twice,
I think I know enough of hate
To say that for destruction ice
Is also great
And would suffice.

沒有給選擇的路

昏黃的樹林裡有兩條叉路，
可惜我不能把兩條都選取。
我在旅行徘徊了許久，
盡力願望著其中的一條，
牠向那矮矮的叢林裡蜿蜒而去。

於是我又望著目標美麗的另外一條，

這條路也許更好，

因為牠還沒有給走壞，還長滿著綠草；

不過關於走過了多少，

這兩條路是在有同樣的消耗，

而且那早晨這兩條路上的綠葉

都不曾給腳步踩黑。

於是啊，我在第一條路上還多走了一天，

可是我知道路是怎樣地引到路，

我懷疑我該不該走回去。

當悠悠的歲月之後在某個地方，

我將歎息著一再地說道：

樹林裡兩條路指向不同的方向，

而我，我選擇了那少走過的一條，

這便一切都成了兩樣。

一九五二年九月十五日

The Road Not Taken

Two roads diverged in a yellow wood,

And sorry I could not travel both

And be one traveler, long I stood
And looked down one as far as I could
To where it bent in the undergrowth;

Then took the other, as just as fair,
And having perhaps the better claim
Because it was grassy and wanted wear,
Though as for that the passing there
Had worn them really about the same,

And both that morning equally lay
In leaves no step had trodden black.
Oh, I marked the first for another day!
Yet knowing how way leads on to way
I doubted if I should ever come back.

I shall be telling this with a sigh
Somewhere ages and ages hence:
Two roads diverged in a wood, and I,
I took the one less traveled by,
And that has made all the difference.

修牆

有些東西不愛一道牆壁，

把牆腳下凍裂的泥土拱脹，

搞翻牆上的石子兒；在陽光

還造成了裂縫，讓兩個人走過還寬鬆

獵人們底工作卻是另一種勾當：

我跟著他們到處去修牆，

不肯讓一塊石頭沒砌在石頭上，

他們要使白兔沒法兒躲藏，

好叫汪汪的獵犬容易追上。

我所說的裂縫是怎樣被造成，

誰也沒看見，誰也沒聽見，

可是到了春天修補的季節，就發現了牠們。

我告訴我鄰居，他住在山那邊；

有一天，我們就回去察看這條防線，

打掉把我們之間的這道牆重建。

我和他分別走牆底兩邊。

石子已落在哪一邊就屬於哪一邊。

有些是塊兒有些幾乎成了球。

要把牠們扶正，我們得念一道符咒：

「不等我們走後，你們可不許動！」

扶了這些石頭讓我們底手指結了繭。

啊，這真是一種別緻的戶外運動，兩個人對玩。

除了這，就什麼意義也說不上：

這地方我們不需要這道牆：

我這邊是個蘋果園，他園裡都是松樹。

我底蘋果樹決不會跑過去

吃掉他底松子，我叫他不必顧慮。

他卻說：「好的籬笆造成好的鄰居。」

春天對於我真是個災害，

我不知能不能把意見塞進他底腦袋：

「為什麼籬笆會造成好的鄰居？

是不是因為這兒有母牛？可是這兒並沒有母牛。

當我去造一道牆，我就早該弄清楚，

我要把什麼圍進或圍出；

我想要和誰相牴觸？

有些東西不愛一道牆，

要把牆推倒。」

我可能叫那鄰居一聲：「妖怪」，

但又不恰是妖怪，我寧願讓他自己去編派。

我見他在那兒雙手緊握著石塊，

像個武裝的舊石器時代的野人，

我想他不但走向樹蔭和黑暗的森林。

而且忘不掉他父親底家訓，

高興把牠記得那麼清清楚楚，

可以說了又說：「好的籬笆造成好的鄰居。」

一九五一年七月二十二日譯於密大

Mending Wall

Something there is that doesn't love a wall,

That sends the frozen-ground-swell under it,

And spills the upper boulders in the sun,

And makes gaps even two can pass abreast.

The work of hunters is another thing:

I have come after them and made repair

Where they have left not one stone on a stone,

But they would have the rabbit out of hiding,

To please the yelping dogs. The gaps I mean,

No one has seen them made or heard them made,

But at spring mending-time we find them there.

I let my neighbor know beyond the hill;

And on a day we meet to walk the line

And set the wall between us once again.

We keep the wall between us as we go.

To each the boulders that have fallen to each.

And some are loaves and some so nearly balls

We have to use a spell to make them balance:

'Stay where you are until our backs are turned!'

We wear our fingers rough with handling them.

Oh, just another kind of out-door game,

One on a side. It comes to little more:

There where it is we do not need the wall:

He is all pine and I am apple orchard.

My apple trees will never get across

And eat the cones under his pines, I tell him.

He only says, 'Good fences make good neighbors'.

Spring is the mischief in me, and I wonder

If I could put a notion in his head:

'Why do they make good neighbors? Isn't it

Where there are cows?

But here there are no cows.

Before I built a wall I'd ask to know

What I was walling in or walling out,

And to whom I was like to give offence.

Something there is that doesn't love a wall,

That wants it down.' I could say 'Elves' to him,

But it's not elves exactly, and I'd rather

He said it for himself. I see him there

Bringing a stone grasped firmly by the top

In each hand, like an old-stone savage armed.

He moves in darkness as it seems to me—

Not of woods only and the shade of trees.

He will not go behind his father's saying,

And he likes having thought of it so well

He says again, "Good fences make good neighbors."

雪夜小駐林邊外

我想我知道這是誰的樹林。
雖然他底家是在那個鄉村;
他不會看到我在這兒停留,
望著他那堆滿冰雪的樹林。

我底小馬兒定會覺得奇怪
怎麼停在不近農家的所在,
當這一年中最晦暗的深宵
在樹林和冰凍之湖的交界。

他把他轡勒上的鈴兒一搖
來問一聲是否有什麼蹊蹺,
此外唯一可以聽到的聲音
是那個輕風與雪片的掠掃。

比較杜牧（803 A.D.—852）：〈山行〉

遠上寒山石徑斜,
白雲深處有人家;
停車坐愛楓林晚,
霜葉紅杉二月花。

　　譯文用韻方式與原作大致相同，而每首第一、二、四句用韻，
第三句與下面的一首同韻。原作每行八個音節，譯文每行十一字。
但原作每行四個重音，譯作大致上每行也可分做四個音步，例如：

我想 我知道 這是誰底 樹<u>林</u>。
雖然 他底家 是在 那個鄉<u>村</u>；
他不會 看到我 在這兒 徘徊，
望著 他那 堆滿冰雪的 樹<u>林</u>。

Stopping By Woods on a Snowy Evening

Whose woods these are I think I know.

His house is in the village though;

He will not see me stopping here

To watch his woods fill up with snow.

My little horse must think it queer

To stop without a farmhouse near

Between the woods and frozen lake

The darkest evening of the year.

He gives his harness bells a shake
To ask if there is some mistake.
The only other sound's the sweep
Of easy wind and downy flake.

The woods are lovely, dark and deep.
But I have promises to keep,
And miles to go before I sleep,
And miles to go before I sleep.

請進

我走到這林子底邊緣，
聽！有隻畫眉在奏樂
這時候外面早已黃昏，
那裡面更是一片漆黑。

這林子實在是太黑了，
小鳥如何把這一切挨過！
牠雖然乖巧也做不好窩，
至多，至多只能唱唱歌。

夕陽的最後一線光芒
眼看就要死滅在西方，
只因牠賴在畫眉底懷裡，
才多活了一個歌兒的時光。

在這樹木陰森的暗處
畫眉的音樂——
仿彿像一個召喚我進去，
到那黑暗裡去自怨自傷

我可要在外面看看星星：
決不願走進這個森林。
就算是千呼萬喚我也不動心
何況你並沒有真正來邀請。

一九五六年四月二十五日夜一時半譯於20 Sumner Road Cambridge, Mass

Come In

As I came to the edge of the woods,
Thrush music—hark!

Now if it was dusk outside,
Inside it was dark.

Too dark in the woods for a bird
By sleight of wing
To better its perch for the night,
Though it still could sing.

The last of the light of the sun
That had died in the west
Still lived for one song more
In a thrush's breast.

Far in the pillared dark
Thrush music went—
Almost like a call to come in
To the dark and lament.

But no, I was out for stars;
I would not come in.
I meant not even if asked;
And I hadn't been.

歐納司・道生（Ernest Dowson）

我已不是賽娜拉管轄下的我了

昨夜，啊，昨夜我和她接吻的時辰，
賽娜拉呀！我想起了你苗條的身影。
在吻和酒的當中，你底氣息印上了我底心靈；
我是多麼淒涼啊，我厭倦了舊情，
是啊，我是多麼淒涼，把頭兒低垂：
賽娜拉呀！我總算對你也夠忠誠，我盡了自己的心。

這一夜我底新緊貼著她熱辣辣跳動的心，
她整夜在我懷裡睡得多麼親；
當然啊，她出賣的鮮紅的嘴唇給我甜吻；
但是當我醒來看見灰暗的黎明，
我是多麼淒涼啊，我厭倦了舊情：
賽娜拉呀！我總算對你也夠忠誠，我盡了自己的心。

我已把往事都遺忘，賽娜拉呀，我隨風飄蕩，
我拋散玫瑰，拋散玫瑰，隨著人群放浪，

舞蹈發狂，好把你慘白凋殘的蓮花不放在心上；

但是我是多麼淒涼啊，我厭倦了舊情，

是啊，我永遠這樣，因為這舞蹈是那麼久長：

賽娜拉呀！我總算對你也夠忠誠，我盡了自己的心。

我高叫著要更瘋狂的音樂，更強烈的美酒，

可是當筵席歇散，燈光熄滅之後，

你底身影卻出沒沉浮，賽娜拉呀！你把這黑夜佔有；

我是多麼淒涼啊，我厭倦了舊情，

是啊，我渴想著我所要的嘴脣：

賽娜拉呀！我總算對你也夠忠誠，我盡了自己的心。

一九五七年七月九日夜十二時

　　這詩拉丁文題目轉引自道生所喜讀的Horace底Odes第四卷之首，意為："I am not what I was under the reign of the lovely Cynara."

Non Sum Qualis Eram Bonae sub Regno Cynarae[1]

Last night, ah, yesternight, betwixt her lips and mine
There fell thy shadow, Cynara! thy breath was shed
Upon my soul between the kisses and the wine;
And I was desolate and sick of an old passion,
Yea, I was desolate and bowed my head:
I have been faithful to thee, Cynara! in my fashion.

All night upon mine heart I felt her warm heart beat,
Night-long within mine arms in love and sleep she lay;
Surely the kisses of her bought red mouth were sweet;
But I was desolate and sick of an old passion,
When I awoke and found the dawn was gray:
I have been faithful to you, Cynara! in my fashion.

I have forgot much, Cynara! gone with the wind,
Flung roses, roses riotously with the throng,
Dancing, to put thy pale, lost lilies out of mind;
But I was desolate and sick of an old passion,
Yea, all the time, because the dance was long;
I have been faithful to thee, Cynara! in my fashion.

I cried for madder music and for stronger wine,

---

[1]　【編者按】：此詩英文原文為編者所加，原書稿缺。

But when the feast is finished and the lamps expire,
Then falls thy shadow, Cynara! the night is thine;
And I am desolate and sick of an old passion,
Yea, hungry for the lips of my desire:
I have been faithful to thee, Cynara! in my fashion.

幽居[1]

你我底幽居是怎樣個地方？
那兒有暗淡的星光
照耀在蘋果花梢
和露水淋漓的葡萄藤上。

那個幽靜的山谷
我們終要尋到，
在那裡再也聽不到
人類的喧囂。

在那裡我們忘掉一切，
也全部被遺忘，

---

[1] 【編者按】：原文書稿缺詩作原文

怡然相得地安息，
深藏在世人不見的地方。
我們已把這世界拋棄，
榮譽和辛勞也不在意，
我們不至發覺
星星會不仁慈。[2]

人們還到處漫遊，
有哭也有笑；
但我們卻幻想著
諸天沉睡，幽夢迢迢。

一個幽靜的境界有暗淡的星光
照耀在蘋果花梢
和露水淋漓的葡萄藤上。願這是你我同住的地方！

一九五七年七月六日下午五時，譯於16 Dunster St.五樓, Cambridge, Mass

---

[2] 【譯者注】「星星」在這兒也許可以做「命星」。

魯巴克（Phyllis M. Lubbock）

「我摘了一枝櫻草」

我摘了一枝慘白的櫻草，
纖弱得像你底手腕，伊麗莎，
陽光在那兒投了一瞥，
像投進你雅麗的頭髮。

我摘了一朵紫羅蘭，
甜蜜得像你嘴脣底呼吸，
它底深暗也像你眼睛下
沉思的紫色影子。

我摘了一枝櫻草，慘白得像死亡——
還有雪白的紫羅蘭，伊麗莎，
這都不及你柔嫩的肌膚美麗無瑕，
也不及我偷偷放進那花兒的地方。

一九五二年八月十八日

I Picked a Primrose

I picked a primrose, pale as death,
Frail as your wrist, Elizabeth,
The sun had left a glimmer there,
As delicate as in your hair.

I picked a violet sweet as breath
That parts your lips, Elizabeth,
And dark as where beneath your eyes
A brooding purple shadow lies.

I picked a primrose pale as death—
White violets too, Elizabeth,
None fairer than your tender skin,
Nor where I slipped the flowers in.

鮑德朗（Francis William Bourdillon）

黑夜有一千隻眼睛

黑夜有一千隻眼睛，
白天只有一個；
可是隨著那落山的太陽
就死去了輝煌的世界之光。

腦有一千隻眼睛，
心只有一個；
可是當愛情已經完結
整個生命之光也就熄滅。

一九五三年五月二十七日

The Night Has A Thousand Eyes

The night has a thousand eyes,

And the day but one;

Yet the light of the bright world dies

With the dying sun.

The mind has a thousand eyes,

And the heart but one:

Yet the light of a whole life dies

When love is done.

濟慈（John Keats）

大地的詩

大地的詩永遠也不死：
當小鳥都怕火熱的太陽，
偷偷躲進樹林裡去乘涼，
柔茵的草坪上有聲音繞著籬笆飛；
這是蚱蜢在歌唱——他趁早迎接
孟夏的豪華——歡喜到
無盡無涯；因為要是玩倦了，
他就會在愉快的草叢裡安憩。

大地的詩從來也不停：
在寂寞的冬夜，當霜花精製了靜默，
灶下卻振動蟋蟀唱歌的翅膀，
他越唱，越唱，越熱情，
使迷離欲睡的人恍惚感覺
蚱蜢底歌還逗留在蔥蘢的小山上。

一九五五年六月三十日夜二時

　　這是濟慈在和人比賽下即席吟成的最美麗的小詩。有一天，在十二月裡，濟慈和早已成名而獎掖他的詩人韓特（Leigh Hunt）坐在爐邊聽蟋蟀，聽這「爐邊快活的小蚱蜢」，韓特提議他們兩人各寫十四行詩一首比賽，主題就是「詠蚱蜢和蟋蟀」。由濟慈從小的朋友克拉克（Cowden Clauhe）記時間，結果濟慈比贏了。韓特寫了一首很美的詩讚頌這田野和爐邊「可愛的小兄弟們，」但濟慈，雖然很謙虛地認為韓特底詩比他自己的要好些，卻實際上達成了他創作完美的效果。這詩運用了濟慈慣用的技巧，把火熱的太陽和涼蔭的樹林對比，襯托並加強了第一行的恬靜性，詩末再回顧到蚱蜢，是一種特別快意的點染女詩人阿密‧勞威爾（Amy Lowell）在傳記裡說：「這結束不僅在技巧上很美，而且從心理狀態上說來也是很美麗的。」這詩在某種已經上似乎可與詩經七月對照。

The Poetry of Earth Is Never Dead

The poetry of earth is never dead:
When all the birds are faint with the hot sun
And hide in cooling trees, a voice will run,
From hedge to hedge about the new-mown mead;
That is the Grasshopper's—he takes the lead
In summer luxury,—he has never done
With his delights; for when tired out with fun
He rests at ease beneath some pleasant weed.

The poetry of earth is ceasing never:

On a lone winter evening, when the frost

Has wrought a silence, from the stove there shrills

The Cricket's song, in warmth increasing ever,

And seems to one in drowsiness half lost,

The Grasshopper's among some grassy hills.

明亮的星呀

明星啊！但願我能像你一般永恆──

並不是要整夜高懸，發出孤寂的光輝，

老睜永恆的眼睛，

像大自然耐心、失眠的隱士，

注視那滾滾常流的碧水

祭司給人海的巖岸寨節沐浴，

或者凝視著那柔軟的新雪

給高山和曠野戴上面具──

我不要像這樣，卻也要永恆不變，

枕著我美麗的愛人成熟的胸脯，

永遠感覺到那溫柔的起伏，

在甜美的不安中無眠，

悄悄地，悄悄地去聽她輕盈的呼吸，

讓我老這門活下去罷——要不，就昏迷至死。

一九五六年六月一日夜十二時譯於 20 Sumner Road Cambridge, Mass

　　一九二〇年，濟慈自知他底肺病一天天加重，想去海濱休養，
仍是無效。他所心愛的芳妮‧白郎（Fanny Brawne）來看護他，但
她底親近和絕望的愛，更加重了他的痛苦。七月裡，他底最後，也
是最好的詩集出版，得到讀者底熱烈歡迎，但已不能有助於他健康
地恢復了。九月間，濟慈乘船去意大利，想藉此休養病體。在和芳
妮最後一別後上船。經過莫吉利海峽時，船遇風浪，被迫駛返魯爾
倭斯灣（Lulworth），他上岸一行與祖國作最後一別，晚上回到船
上後就寫了「明星啊」這首十四行詩。這詩寫在一本莎士比亞詩集
的面對著長詩「愛人底哀愁」（A Lover's Complaint）的空頁上，
是他底絕筆詩，四個月之後他就死於羅馬，卒年二十五歲。

〔附〕袁水拍譯：

「明亮的星呀，如果我能像你一樣久長！」為什麼詩人追求者不可
能的事呢？因為這是詩的主要功用，牠是從魔術發展出來的。飢餓
而受驚的蠻族為痴為狂地跳著模擬性的舞，在強烈的精神與肉體的
瘋狂機動中，他們失去了對外面真實世界的意識，而墮入下意識

中，幻想的內心世界中，這一幻想世界是他們所希望要達到的。他
們企圖以意志的力量，把幻想去影響現實。在這裡他們是失敗了，
可是所付的力氣不是白費的。因為他們和他們的環境之間的矛盾，
現在是解決了。平衡再又恢復。因此，當他們重新回到現實世界來
時，他們實際上確是比過去更適合與現實搏鬥了。……

「明亮的星呀，如果我能像你一樣久長！」這是他（濟慈）的願望
───一個垂死的病人的願望。但其中充滿著詩的回憶：

可是我和北極星一樣堅定，
牠的固守和久遠的性質，
在天空中再也找不出別個。

好像彈簧放開一樣，他的想象活動起來了。他把自己比做星，再比
做月。人類歷史從開頭起，月就被作為永久的生命的象徵，而成為
神祕的膜拜對象。他還意識到那隻船輕輕地搖擺，跟著海浪駛進灣
去。他設想自己是月亮，俯視潮水怎樣在地平線上吞吐舒卷：

「不像那天空的忍耐而失眠的隱士，
高懸天際發出孤獨的光芒，永遠睜開永恆的眼皮，
或者注視著山峰和曠野
所蓋著的柔軟的新雪的面幕，
那常流的碧水卻像教士一般
洗滌著人間的海岸。」

這樣他沉入永恆之中，依舊受著船的催眠性的搖擺，他回到世上：

「不，還是那樣固定，還是沒有變換，

枕著我愛人的成熟的胸脯，

永遠感到那溫柔的起伏，

在甘美的不安中醒過來，

依舊聽到她的輕盈的呼吸，

讓我永遠這樣活下去——

可是這是不可能的。沒有死亡得不到愛情。

讓我永遠這樣活下去，否則昏迷死亡。」

他醒了。這像是被船的搖擺所擾亂的夢。但是在這場夢裡，他拋開
了壓迫他的東西。他重新恢復了平靜的心境。世界還是那客觀上相
同的世界——這世界，青年漸漸蒼老、消瘦、死亡——
可是他對他的主觀態度已經改變。因此，對於他說，已經不再是原
來的了。這就是詩的辯證法，也是魔術的辯證法。

——喬治・湯姆生著，袁水拍譯：《馬克思主義與詩歌》（北京：
生活・讀書・新知三新書店，一九五〇年出版，原係一九四三年，
馬克思逝世六十週年，方始出版的紀念叢書之一），第一章，「語
言和魔術，」頁十九－二十三。

"Bright star, would I were stedfast as thou art"[1]

Bright star, would I were stedfast as thou art—
    Not in lone splendour hung aloft the night
And watching, with eternal lids apart,
    Like nature's patient, sleepless Eremite,
The moving waters at their priestlike task
    Of pure ablution round earth's human shores,
Or gazing on the new soft-fallen mask
    Of snow upon the mountains and the moors—
No—yet still stedfast, still unchangeable,
    Pillow'd upon my fair love's ripening breast,
To feel for ever its soft fall and swell,
    Awake for ever in a sweet unrest,
Still, still to hear her tender-taken breath,
And so live ever—or else swoon to death.

---

[1] 【編者按】：此詩英文原文為編者所加，原書稿缺。

希臘古瓶歌

1

你白璧無瑕的恬靜姑娘，

沉默和悠閒把你撫養，

你田園的史家，能說個開花的故事

比我們底詩歌說得更甜蜜：

這是什麼綠葉繡邊的軼事

繚繞著你仙凡的形跡，

在風光明媚的鄧樸或阿客蒂山谷？

這是什麼凡人或神仙？是什麼姑娘在不願？

是什麼瘋狂的追求？是什麼掙扎和逃拒？

是什麼簫鼓，又是什麼狂歡？

2

沒聽見的樂曲比聽見了的更可愛，

所以柔和的簫笛啊請你吹奏：

不要奏給我敏感的耳朵，

更惹人愛得，請奏個無聲的心靈小曲：

樹林下美麗的少年你離不了你底歌，

這綠葉永遠也不會凋落；

勇敢的愛人呀你從來也不能接吻，

雖然已和這目標接近──但你也不用憂心；

你雖然還沒贏得她底垂青，但她用不凋零，

你將永遠愛她，她也永遠美麗媚人。

3

啊，歡樂的，歡樂的樹枝！

你葉兒長青，和春天永不分手；

還有這歡樂的吹奏者你說不厭倦，

永遠吹奏著常新的歌曲；

更多的歡戀！更多更多的歡戀！

永遠熱情，使心花怒放，

永遠要求，也永遠年芳；

詠味著遠高於人慾的慾望，

給心靈高超的憂鬱和滿足，

煽起周邊的情焰，把脣舌燒枯。

4

這來獻祭的是什麼人們？

神祕的祭司啊，這小犢牛仔仰天哀吟，

柔軟的腰身美飾著花綵繽紛，

你牽她到什麼綠色的祭壇去犧牲？

這河邊或海濱是什麼市鎮，

矗立在山頭的是什麼平靜的衛城，

怎這般萬人空巷，在這虔誠的早晨？

小鎮啊，你底街巷將永遠寂靜；

找不到一個人兒來說明

為什麼你這般荒涼，沒喚回半個人影。

5

啊，雅典的風姿！美麗的儀態！

這兒有白玉的少年和姑娘，濃妝著綵帶，

有繁枝和殘草點綴著光彩；

靜默的形影啊，你是曲「清冷的牧歌」！

你像「永恆」一樣，逗得我們不能想像。

當歲月快使這青春消瘦，

你卻禁得住異樣的哀愁，

永遠是人底好友，

你對他說：「美就是真，真就是美——

這就是你所知的和要知的真理。」

一九五七年元旦夜十二時譯於20 Sumner Road Cambridge, Mass

Ode on a Grecian URN

1

Thou still unravish'd bride of quietness,

Thou foster-child of silence and slow time,

Sylvan historian, who canst thus express

A flowery tale more sweetly than our rhyme:

What leaf-fringed legend haunts about thy shape

Of deities or mortals, or of both,

In Tempe or the dales of Arcady?

What men or gods are these? What maidens loth?

What mad pursuit? What struggle to escape?

What pipes and timbrels? What wild ecstasy?

2

Heard melodies are sweet, but those unheard

Are sweeter; therefore, ye soft pipes, play on;

Not to the sensual ear, but, more endeared,

Pipe to the spirit ditties of no tone:

Fair youth, beneath the trees, thou canst not leave

Thy song, nor ever can those trees be bare;

Bold Lover, never, never canst thou kiss,

Though winning near the goal—yet, do not grieve;

She cannot fade, though thou hast not thy bliss,

For ever wilt thou love, and she be fair!

3

Ah, happy, happy boughs! that cannot shed

Your leaves, nor ever bid the Spring adieu;

And, happy melodist, unwearied,

For ever piping songs for ever new;

More happy love! more happy, happy love!

For ever warm and still to be enjoyed,

For ever panting and for ever young;

All breathing human passion far above,

That leaves a heart high-sorrowful and cloyed,

A burning forehead, and a parching tongue.

4

Who are these coming to the sacrifice?

To what green altar, O mysterious priest,

Lead'st thou that heifer lowing at the skies,

And all her silken flanks with garlands drest?

What little town by river or sea-shore,

Or mountain-built with peaceful citadel,

Is emptied of its folk, this pious morn?

And, little town, thy streets for evermore

Will silent be; and not a soul to tell

Why thou art desolate, can e'er return.

5

O Attic shape! Fair attitude! with brede

Of marble men and maidens overwrought,

With forest branches and the trodden weed;

Thou, silent form, dost tease us out of thought

As doth eternity. Cold pastoral!

When old age shall this generation waste,

Thou shalt remain, in midst of other woe

Than ours, a friend to man, to whom thou say'st,

"Beauty is truth, truth beauty, —that is all

Ye know on earth, and all ye need to know."

繆蕾爾・魯克色（**Muriel Rukeyser**）

歌

世界充滿了失敗；風啊，請把愛帶給我，
我底家就是我們會見的地方。
不管我在那臉上會觸到和聽到什麼
請把愛帶給我。

風呵，請從我眼裡吹掉流亡；
給我和平的希望，生命的消息和懺悔，
給我自由去尋，去尋，去尋
那赤子之心。

一九五六年四月二十三日夜二時譯於20 Sumner Road, Cambridge, Mass

Song

The world is full of loss; bring, wind, my love,
My home is where we make our meeting-place,
And love whatever I shall touch and read
Within that face.

Lift, wind, my exile from my eyes;
Pease to look, life to listen and confess,
Freedom to find to find to find
That nakedness.

懷阿特（Sir Thomas Wyatt）[1]

給一位女郎的最後通牒[2]

女郎啊，我不想多說，
只要知道你願意麼；
你如果願意，就請別開心，
用你底智慧說出真心；
因為只要你向我一招手就行。
要是對一個老是給熱情燒傷的人
你還有幾分憐惜和同情，
就該明白地對他說個是或不：
如果是個是，我會歡喜點頭；
如果是個不，還一樣是朋友；
不過你將找到另外一個人，
而我還屬於我自己，再也不歸你所有。

一九五三年二月二十一日

---

[1]　【編者按】：詩人英文名為編者所加，原稿缺。
[2]　【編者按】：原稿缺詩作原文。

蘭德（Walter Savage Landor）

死

死神在我之上，向我耳邊
低聲說了些我不解的話；
在他那離奇的語言裡，我只懂得一點，
那兒沒有一句可怕的話。

另譯：

死

天風一夕召吾魂，
帝墜吾前耳語沉；
萬句迷離惟一悟——
了無一語可驚心。

一九四〇年譯於重慶

Death

Death stands above me, whispering low
I know not what into my ear;
Of his strange language all I know
Is, there is not a word of fear.

你底名字

我明明記得你怎樣微笑著
看著我把你底名字寫在柔軟的海沙上。
「喲！你真是個孩子喲！
你滿以為是寫在石頭上！」
自從那次我把它寫上，
湖水永遠洗它不滅；
後世的人們在無邊的海洋
到處都能讀到哀安思底小名。

一九五五年七月十五日夜一時半

Well I Remember How You Smiled

Well I remember how you smiled
To see me write your name upon
The soft sea-sand . "O! what a child!
You think you're writing upon stone!"
I have since written what no tide
Shall ever wash away, what men
Unborn shall read o'er ocean wide
And find Ianthe's name again.

為什麼

為什麼我們失去了歡情
讓煩憂來抓住心？
我實在不知。造物者說了一聲
「服從」；人就服從了。
我眼見荊棘叢生，薔薇死，
卻不知是什麼道理。

Why

Why do our joys depart

For cares to seize the heart?

I know not. Nature says,

Obey; and man obeys.

I see, and know not why,

Thorns live and roses die.

無名氏（Anonymous）

義務

我夢到生命就是「美」；
醒來卻發覺牠是「義務」。
難道你底夢是個朦朧的謊？
憂愁的心呵，英勇地勞動下去，
你就會發現你底夢原來是
光天化日下的光，對你全是真理。

一九五五年六月二十九日夜十二時

Duty

I slept, and dreamed that life was beauty;
I woke, and found that life was duty.

Was thy dream then a shadowy lie?
Toil on, sad heart, courageously,
And thou shall find thy dream to be
A noonday light and truth to thee.

戀歌（約1600年作）

我愛她底衣裳穿得聰明，
是那麼適當，衣和人簡直不能分；
年年季季都打扮得合身，
無論是春夏秋冬的時辰。
穿上所有的衣裳，
對她底美好無所損；
脫光了所有的衣裳，
她更是「美」底本身。

一九五六年四月二十三日下午八時譯於20 Sumner Road, Cambridge, Mass

Madrigal (c.1600 A.D)

My Love in her attire doth show her wit,

It doth so well become her;

For every season she hath dressings fit,

For Winter, Spring, and Summer.

No beauty she doth miss

When all her robes are on;

But Beauty's self she is

When all her robes are gone.

後記

黎漢傑

　　我是很晚才知道周公的名字的，那時他已經仙逝多年，遺憾不曾有機會當面聆聽教益。而說到真正認識、瞭解這位當代的漢學家，就要數幾年前，機運巧合，從事周先生的書信整理工作，才開始的。工作前後兩年，我一直流連在香港浸會大學圖書館特藏部，在周公的專屬檔案櫃翻箱倒籠，看著一封封泛黃的紙片、褪色的筆墨，談詩、論文；說世事、說人情，好像和周公重新經歷了一趟生命之旅。之後，研究計畫結束，我提交了文字檔案，一般而言，這就意味研究者與研究對象的關係告一段落。可是，也許天意有所安排，後來在香港一位長輩家裡，看到周公寫的字畫，還有親筆題贈的現代詩集《海燕》，才驚覺原來周公與我的距離，好像一點都不遙遠。每次見面，我們都會談起周公，有時幾句，有時一席話，像香，淡淡的，時不時跌宕一點餘韻。年前，王潤華老師傳來周先生的書稿《風媒集》，商議一起合作編輯將之出版，我立刻答應了，心想這又能延續和周公的緣分，亦是一生一大樂事。過程之中，幾位老師分處各地，大家只能以書信聯絡，往回多次，解答我不少疑難與困惑。也許，老一輩人比較重感情，多年以後，幾位老師還一直心心念念，出版先生的遺稿，還在百忙中，親自幫忙編輯、校對，希望這次出版，能為周公的翻譯事業，作一個補白。

讀詩人102　PG1667

 風媒集：
周策縱翻譯詩集

譯　　著	周策縱
編　　者	心笛、王潤華、瘂弦、黎漢傑
責任編輯	洪仕翰
圖文排版	周妤靜
封面設計	蔡瑋筠

出版策劃	釀出版
製作發行	秀威資訊科技股份有限公司
	114 台北市內湖區瑞光路76巷65號1樓
	電話：+886-2-2796-3638　傳真：+886-2-2796-1377
	服務信箱：service@showwe.com.tw
	http://www.showwe.com.tw
郵政劃撥	19563868　戶名：秀威資訊科技股份有限公司
展售門市	國家書店【松江門市】
	104 台北市中山區松江路209號1樓
	電話：+886-2-2518-0207　傳真：+886-2-2518-0778
網路訂購	秀威網路書店：http://www.bodbooks.com.tw
	國家網路書店：http://www.govbooks.com.tw
法律顧問	毛國樑　律師
總 經 銷	聯合發行股份有限公司
	231新北市新店區寶橋路235巷6弄6號4F
	電話：+886-2-2917-8022　傳真：+886-2-2915-6275

出版日期	2017年1月　BOD一版
定　　價	420元

國家圖書館出版品預行編目

風媒集：周策縱翻譯詩集 / 周策縱譯著, 心笛等編.
-- 一版. -- 臺北市：釀出版, 2017.01
　　面；　公分. -- (讀詩人；102)
　BOD版
　ISBN 978-986-445-172-2(平裝)

813.1   105022009

讀者回函卡

感謝您購買本書，為提升服務品質，請填妥以下資料，將讀者回函卡直接寄回或傳真本公司，收到您的寶貴意見後，我們會收藏記錄及檢討，謝謝！
如您需要了解本公司最新出版書目、購書優惠或企劃活動，歡迎您上網查詢或下載相關資料：http:// www.showwe.com.tw

您購買的書名：＿＿＿＿＿＿＿＿＿＿＿＿＿＿＿＿＿＿＿＿＿＿＿＿

出生日期：＿＿＿＿年＿＿＿＿月＿＿＿＿日

學歷：□高中 (含) 以下　　□大專　　□研究所 (含) 以上

職業：□製造業　□金融業　□資訊業　□軍警　□傳播業　□自由業
　　　□服務業　□公務員　□教職　　□學生　□家管　□其它＿＿＿＿

購書地點：□網路書店　□實體書店　□書展　□郵購　□贈閱　□其他

您從何得知本書的消息？

　□網路書店　□實體書店　□網路搜尋　□電子報　□書訊　□雜誌

　□傳播媒體　□親友推薦　□網站推薦　□部落格　□其他＿＿＿＿＿＿

您對本書的評價：(請填代號　1.非常滿意　2.滿意　3.尚可　4.再改進)

　封面設計＿＿＿　版面編排＿＿＿　內容＿＿＿　文／譯筆＿＿＿　價格＿＿＿

讀完書後您覺得：

□很有收穫　□有收穫　□收穫不多　□沒收穫

對我們的建議：＿＿＿＿＿＿＿＿＿＿＿＿＿＿＿＿＿＿＿＿＿＿＿＿

＿＿＿＿＿＿＿＿＿＿＿＿＿＿＿＿＿＿＿＿＿＿＿＿＿＿＿＿＿＿＿＿

＿＿＿＿＿＿＿＿＿＿＿＿＿＿＿＿＿＿＿＿＿＿＿＿＿＿＿＿＿＿＿＿

＿＿＿＿＿＿＿＿＿＿＿＿＿＿＿＿＿＿＿＿＿＿＿＿＿＿＿＿＿＿＿＿

11466

台北市內湖區瑞光路 76 巷 65 號 1 樓

秀威資訊科技股份有限公司　　　收

BOD 數位出版事業部

··

（請沿線對折寄回，謝謝！）

姓　　名：＿＿＿＿＿＿＿＿　年齡：＿＿＿＿　性別：□女　□男

郵遞區號：□□□□□

地　　址：＿＿＿＿＿＿＿＿＿＿＿＿＿＿＿＿＿＿＿

聯絡電話：(日) ＿＿＿＿＿＿＿＿＿　(夜) ＿＿＿＿＿＿＿＿＿

E-mail：＿＿＿＿＿＿＿＿＿＿＿＿＿＿＿＿＿＿＿